SPECIAL DELIVERY

"What is it?" Tori asked.

Startled, her mother pulled a sheet of paper out of the envelope and hastily dropped the envelope into the wastepaper basket. "Nothing, Tori, just something for work." She turned away and opened the sheet of writing paper.

From where she was standing, Tori could see her mother's shoulders tighten as she read the letter. Abruptly she folded the paper and slid it into the pocket of her robe.

"Well!" Mrs. Carsen said brightly, turning to face Tori. "This is the big day, isn't it? You'll have to eat a good breakfast, Tori. I'll take a shower, and we'll go down to the restaurant. Think about your program while you're waiting," she added as she bustled into the bathroom.

Mystified, Tori walked over to the wastepaper basket and fished around for the envelope. Printed neatly and clearly in the center of the envelope were the words *Miss Tori Carsen*.

It was for me, Tori thought, amazed. But why wouldn't Mom let me see it?

THE
COMPETITION

Melissa Lowell

Created by Parachute Press

A SKYLARK BOOK

NEW YORK · TORONTO · LONDON · SYDNEY · AUCKLAND

RL 5.2, 009–012

THE COMPETITION
A Skylark Book / January 1994

Skylark Books is a registered trademark of Bantam Books, a division of Bantam Doubleday Dell Publishing Group, Inc. Registered in U.S. Patent and Trademark Office and elsewhere.

ISBN 0-553-48136-3

Published simultaneously in the United States and Canada

Bantam Books are published by Bantam Books, a division of Bantam Doubleday Dell Publishing Group, Inc. Its trademark, consisting of the words "Bantam Books" and the portrayal of a rooster, is Registered in U.S. Patent and Trademark Office and in other countries. Marca Registrada. Bantam Books, 1540 Broadway, New York, New York 10036.

PRINTED IN THE UNITED STATES OF AMERICA

OPM 0 9 8 7 6 5

1

"**T**wo days!"

Tori Carsen pivoted on the ice to see who had shouted out those words. Scattered across the rink at the Seneca Hills Ice Arena were several skaters practicing parts of their programs. Sixteen-year-old Diana Mitchell was at one end of the oval, her bright red hair flying, holding up two fingers. Diana shouted out again, "Two days!"

No wonder Diana is excited, Tori thought. She's the best skater in Silver Blades. She'll probably win a medal in the senior ladies' division. But I won't even get to go to the competition at all.

It was two days until the North Atlantic Regional Competition in Lake Placid, New York, and eight of the twenty-six members of Seneca Hills' Silver Blades skating club were going. Tori had thought she'd be one of them—until her mother had broken the news a few days before.

Tori had been a skater and a member of Silver Blades since she was eight years old. Silver Blades was one of the best figure-skating clubs in the country. The members of the club practiced twice a day, every day except Sunday, starting at five-thirty in the morning. They were coached by Franz Weiler, who years earlier had won a silver medal at the Olympics, and Kathy Bart, nicknamed "Sarge" because she was so demanding. Before she stopped competing, Kathy had placed fourth in the Nationals, the most important annual competition in the United States.

Tori skidded to a halt at the side of the rink and brushed a lock of curly blond hair from her blue eyes. She was small for her age—thirteen—and petite. She wore a light-blue skating dress, even though this was only a practice session. Most of the other skaters wore leggings, T-shirts, or warm-up clothes, but Tori always dressed up whenever she skated. Her mother had taught her that wearing beautiful skating outfits would help Tori to skate as if she were performing in front of an audience, even when it was only practice.

"Two days, Tori!" someone else yelled. Spinning around, Tori saw Jill Wong speeding across the ice, her long, dark braid tied with a ribbon in her favorite color, bright red. Jill was Chinese, with dark, solemn eyes framed by black bangs. With Jill were Nikki

Simon and Danielle Panati. Nikki was thin with green eyes, wavy brown hair, freckles across her nose, and braces on her teeth. Danielle had thick, shoulder-length honey-brown hair, large brown eyes, and a slightly stocky body.

The three girls were Tori's best friends in Silver Blades. Jill, Nikki, and Danielle were seventh-graders, too, though they attended Grandview Middle School and Tori went to Kent Academy, a private school in the nearby town of Burgess.

Tori forced herself to smile as she waited for them to skate toward her. She hadn't told them yet that she might not be competing in Lake Placid. She'd been praying for a miracle to occur, but so far that hadn't happened.

"Two days!" Jill said again as she and the other two came to a stop next to Tori. "Can you believe it? In two days we'll be in Lake Placid, New York. North Atlantic Regionals, here we come!"

It just isn't fair, Tori thought. She was the best skater of the four. Well, maybe Jill was a little better, but Tori knew she could outskate her in the junior ladies' division of the competition. If only she could get the chance.

Jill was so excited about the upcoming competition, she couldn't keep still. She skated in tight circles around her friends, waving two fingers to everybody else on the ice.

"Slow down, Jill." Danielle smiled. "You're so hyper!"

"Yeah," said Nikki. She grinned at Jill. "What's the big deal, anyway? I mean, it's *only* the Regional competition."

"Only?" Jill spun to a stop, looking totally shocked. "What do you mean, *only* the Regional? Whoever's in the top four in Lake Placid goes on to the Sectionals, and the top four from that go to the Nationals, and then—"

"I know, I know," Nikki broke in, laughing. "And the top three from the Nationals go to the Worlds or Olympics. I was kidding, Jill."

"I'm so nervous," Danielle said with a shiver. "And I'm really glad you're going to be there, Nikki."

"I wouldn't miss it," Nikki said. "And my mom said I could go since school is closed that week for winter break. I've got to see you guys skate, even if I'm not competing myself."

Tori couldn't help feeling a little sorry for Nikki. Nikki had started out as a singles skater like the rest of them, but then her coach, Kathy Bart, had suggested that she try pairs. Tori didn't think she could ever skate with a partner—it was hard enough just worrying about her own skating. Still, Nikki seemed to like it. She and her partner, Alex Beekman, were doing well, but they weren't ready for competition yet.

"I want to cheer Silver Blades on," Nikki added, "and so does Alex. If you see anybody jumping up and down like crazy and waving pom-poms, that'll be us."

"Just don't wave them during my programs," Jill

warned with a laugh. "My triple toe loop might turn into a triple toe flop." She was skating around the other three again.

"You're awfully quiet, Tori," Danielle commented. "Is something wrong?"

Tori nodded. "Something major," she said. "I might not be going to Lake Placid."

Everybody's mouth dropped open, and Jill stopped skating so abruptly, she bumped into Nikki. "Not going?" Nikki cried. "You're not going?"

"Why not?" Danielle asked, her brown eyes wide with surprise.

"My mother has a big fashion show coming up," Tori said with a groan. Mrs. Carsen was a successful fashion designer. "She's going crazy with designs and last-minute fittings and stuff, and she might not be able to leave the office to take me."

"That's ridiculous!" Jill said bluntly. "Your mother cares more about your skating than her fashion business."

"I thought so, too," Tori agreed. "But every time I try to talk to her about it, I can't get anywhere. She changes the subject or walks away. All she says is, 'There'll be other competitions.' "

"Sure, but you're ready for this one now," Nikki said.

"Other competitions?" Jill snorted. "This is the most important one in our careers so far. I can't believe your mother would actually let you miss it. Other mothers maybe. But not yours!"

Privately Tori agreed. Her mother was definitely *not* the kind to sit back and watch. In fact, she pushed and criticized whenever she got the chance. Tori's father had left her mother when Tori was only six months old, and Tori and her skating had become the top priorities in her mother's life. It just wasn't like Mrs. Carsen to be so casual about a competition. But what could Tori do?

"Look," she said, "I don't like it, but my mother won't change her mind."

"I don't get it," Jill said. "Have you tried to convince her?"

"Of course!" Tori snapped. She didn't like having to defend herself—or her mother—to Jill. "Don't you think I want to go? I know how important it is!"

"Then do something!" Jill snapped back. "You're just giving up."

"Hey, you guys, what's the shouting about?" Melinda Daly, another Silver Blades member who was going to the competition, asked as she skated by. "I could hear you all the way at the other end of the rink." When no one answered her, she frowned and skated away.

Tori brushed back her blond hair with her hand and straightened the hem of her blue skating dress. Jill fiddled with her braid. They didn't look at each other. "We shouldn't be arguing," Danielle said quietly. "What we should be doing is figuring out a way for Tori to go."

"Right!" Nikki said. "There's got to be a way. Come on, you two, stop arguing and start thinking."

Jill grinned at Tori, and Tori smiled back. "Okay," she said, "but you know my mother. If she says she's too busy to drive me to Lake Placid—"

"I've got it!" Jill cut in, snapping her fingers. "She doesn't have to drive you. She doesn't even have to come. You can ride on the bus with the rest of us."

"Of course," Nikki said. "The club's chartered a bus. There'll be room, I bet."

Danielle was already counting. "Jill, me, Diana, Bobby Rodgers, Melinda, Jamie Ross, Gary Hernandez, that's the seven who're competing. And you, Tori, that makes eight. Plus Nikki and Alex. Plus the two coaches. That's only twelve," she said. "And not everybody's mom or dad is coming. Nikki's right, Tori. There'll be plenty of room."

"That's great," said Tori. "But I can't see my mom letting me go without an adult."

"My mom will be there," Jill said. "And so will Mrs. Panati. Tell your mom that there will be plenty of chaperones."

Tori was beginning to feel more hopeful. "Maybe I can talk my mother into it," she said.

"So go tell your mom," Jill said, pointing to the bleachers.

Tori saw her mother walking to a seat in the bleachers, a styrofoam cup in one hand.

Mrs. Carsen was a slender woman with long ash-blond hair. She was always beautifully dressed. This morning she wore dark-blue silk pants with a matching blazer and a cashmere coat thrown over her shoulders.

"What are you doing, Tori?" Mrs. Carsen called out in her loud, raspy voice. "You've got five more minutes before your lesson. You should be working."

Tori came to a stop at the barrier. "I know, Mom, but listen . . ."

"Work on the triple some more," Mrs. Carsen commanded as if she hadn't heard Tori at all. "You should have it down by the next competition so you can really give Jill a run for her money."

"That's what I want to talk to you about," Tori said.

Mrs. Carsen set down her cup. "The triple?" she said. "Tori, the only reason you can't do it yet is because you're not concentrating. Franz doesn't agree of course." She sniffed, mentioning Tori's coach, Franz Weiler. "He says it's going fine and it's just a matter of time before you land it, but I know he's wrong. You've simply got to work harder at it."

Mrs. Carsen took a breath, and Tori jumped in. "I don't want to talk about the triple," she said. "I want to talk about Lake Placid. I've figured out a way I can go!" Excitedly Tori told her mother about the bus ride, and Mrs. Wong's being able to look after her, and how perfectly it would work out. "Isn't that great?" she said.

"In two days I'll be skating in the Regionals. I might actually win a medal!"

Not a single strand of Mrs. Carsen's ash-blond hair was out of place, but she smoothed it anyway. Then she took a sip of tea.

"Isn't that great?" Tori said again. "You can stay here for your fashion show, and I can go to Lake Placid."

"Well." Mrs. Carsen cleared her throat and took another sip from her cup. "I don't think it's quite fair to Mrs. Wong," she said.

Tori frowned. Since when did her mother worry about Mrs. Wong—or anyone for that matter? Her mother cared only about Tori's skating. And Tori's winning. "Mrs. Wong won't mind, you know she won't," Tori said. "Mom, this is my chance to win a medal in the Regionals!"

"Not if you don't start working harder," Mrs. Carsen said.

"How can you say that?" Tori asked. "You're always here watching me. You know how hard I've been working."

"Let's not argue, Tori," Mrs. Carsen said. "You're wasting valuable warm-up time."

Tori wanted to scream. She'd been arriving at the arena by five-fifteen A.M., fifteen minutes earlier in the mornings, just to get some extra time in the weight room and build her leg muscles. A couple of months earlier she'd mastered the double flip jump—a backward takeoff and two full revolutions in the air—and now it was almost second nature to her. She never complained when Mr. Weiler told her to do something over and over again. For two months she'd done nothing but work to get ready for Lake Placid.

"What's the use?" Tori said angrily. "Why should I bother to warm up and work hard if I can't even go to my first important competition?" She felt tears rising to her eyes. She struggled to push them away, but she knew her mother had seen them. "Mom," Tori said quietly, "you know how important this is to me."

Mrs. Carsen stared silently at her tea. Then she looked up and smoothed her hair again. "If you want to be ready for Lake Placid," she said, "then you'd better get moving."

Tori wasn't sure she'd heard right. "You mean I can go?"

Frowning, Mrs. Carsen nodded her head. "But not on the bus," she said curtly. "I'll drive you."

"But what about your show?"

"I'll take care of it," Mrs. Carsen said.

Tori grinned. "That's great, Mom! Thanks!" She started to skate away, but her mother's voice stopped her.

"Just remember, Tori," Mrs. Carsen called out. "You're the one who insisted on going. I expect you to prove that it's worth it." She paused and added, "I expect you to win."

2

Two days later Tori stood in the parking lot of the Seneca Hills Arena and looked around. The place was packed, not just with skaters wearing the light-blue-and-white Silver Blades warm-up jackets, but with families and friends coming to wish them luck and see them off.

Jill's entire family was there, even though only her mother was traveling with her to Lake Placid. Jill had six younger brothers and sisters, and now the two littlest Wong children were jumping all over Jill as if they didn't want to let her leave. Jill was laughing and trying to talk to Danielle at the same time. Mrs. Wong was giving last-minute instructions to the other children.

A big family like that must be a lot of trouble, Tori

told herself. It's always so noisy, and you never get any privacy. But deep down she knew she was jealous. It was always just Tori and her mother. It looked like fun to have so many brothers and sisters.

Over by the big bus Tori spotted Nikki saying good-bye to her parents. The Simons had recently moved to Seneca Hills from Missouri, but Mr. and Mrs. Simon already seemed to know a lot of the other parents.

Next to them stood Danielle and her family, including her grandmother and her older brother, Nicholas. Nicholas looked a lot like Danielle except for his hair, which was spiky and brown. He played ice hockey for the Seneca Hills Hawks, who practiced on the ice arena's other rink. He was in the eighth grade—only one year older than we are, Tori thought. But he always acts as if he's so much cooler. He stood a little bit apart from Danielle and her parents.

"Tori, hi!" Jill suddenly called out, raising her hand and waving Tori over.

"What are you doing here?" Nikki asked when Tori reached them. "I thought your mother was driving you."

"She is, but she wanted to stop and talk to Mr. Weiler," Tori said. She looked toward the arena entrance, where her mother was talking very seriously with Franz Weiler, Tori's coach. He was a short, balding man in a tweed overcoat. "We'll be leaving in a few minutes."

"We were just talking about the Blade Runners,"

Danielle said, "and how we want to beat them."

The Blade Runners, a skating club from Vermont, would be Silver Blades' fiercest rival in the Regional. The Blade Runners were known as a club with great skaters, and they usually took home at least one medal in competitions.

Tori tossed her head. "They're not that good," she said. "Don't you remember last year? Sandy Bower actually fell twice. And her program was so simple, a five-year-old could do it."

"Yeah, but Carla Benson didn't fall," Jill reminded her.

"She's good, huh?" Nikki asked.

"I hate to admit it, but she is," Jill said. "I just hope she's not ready to do a triple yet. I'll have a better chance of beating her if she isn't."

"Carla's so tacky," Tori said, rolling her eyes. "Last time I saw her skate, she actually had white feathers in her hair. She looked like a chicken."

"Yeah, but she skated great," Jill pointed out.

"Let's face it," Danielle said, "every club wants to be the one to bring back the most medals."

Tori sniffed. It would be nice if Silver Blades won the most medals, she guessed. And she hoped that her friends would win. But the most important thing was for *her* to bring back a medal and get her career going.

Just then Kathy Bart appeared. Under a hooded parka she wore her coaching uniform: a Silver Blades jacket, matching blue warm-up pants, and her long dark-blond hair pulled back in a ponytail. She pulled a whistle from her pocket and blew a few piercing shrieks. "Okay, everybody!" she shouted. "We'll be rolling in about ten minutes, so if you haven't loaded your gear, do it now!"

Laughing and chattering, people surged toward the bus and stuffed duffel bags and suitcases into the open baggage compartment. Those who'd already loaded their things turned to say good-bye, and there were shouts of "Good luck" and "We'll keep our fingers crossed" all over the parking lot.

Mrs. Carsen was still talking to Mr. Weiler, so Tori walked toward the bus with the rest of the crowd.

"It's too bad you're not riding with us, Tori," Danielle said. "My grandmother baked pastries last night so we can stuff ourselves on the way."

"I don't think I could eat them," Tori said, wrinkling her nose. "Not on the bus anyway. Those fumes are about ready to make me gag." She looked up at the bus. "I hope the seats recline, or you guys are going to be wiped out by the time you get there."

Bobby Rodgers, a ninth-grader who was standing next to her, laughed. "The seats recline," he told her. Then he pointed to Mrs. Carsen's sleek silver Jaguar parked at the other end of the lot. "Of course, they're not leather like the ones in your mother's Jag. . . ."

Tori smiled. It was a beautiful car, and her friends were always admiring it.

"Why don't you trade places with Tori?" Jill suggested with a grin. "Then Tori can ride with us."

Bobby glanced over at Tori's mother, who looked like she was arguing with Mr. Weiler. "No, thanks." He smirked. "I'll stick with the bus."

Annoyed, Tori turned to say something to Nikki. But Nikki was busy saying good-bye to her parents. Then Jill started hugging everybody in her family and promising to bring each of the kids a memento from Lake Placid. Next to the Wongs, Danielle reached out to take a shopping bag full of pastry and Italian bread from her grandmother.

Tori felt left out again.

Another ear-splitting blast from Kathy's whistle broke into Tori's thoughts, and then Kathy hollered that it was time to go. There was a last flurry of hugs and good-byes before the skaters and those who were traveling with them started boarding the bus.

"Bye, Tori!" Jill hollered. "See you in about six hours!"

Tori waved to her friends, then turned and walked back alone to the car. I'm really glad I have such a nice, comfortable car to ride in, she decided. She'd get to Lake Placid rested and ready to win. And winning was what counted.

"Tori, have you been listening?" Mrs. Carsen guided the car into the right lane of the highway, then glanced over at her daughter. "You keep staring out the window. I can't tell if you even hear me or not."

Reluctantly Tori took her eyes off the thick forest of pine trees sweeping by outside. "I'm listening, Mom," she said. She reached into the glove compartment for some Life Savers and put a red one in her mouth. "You were telling me how important the competition is."

"Yes. In Silver Blades you're close to the top. Jill's your only real competition. But this is a Regional, and you'll be up against some other very good skaters." Tori's mother glanced at her again. "Carla Benson, for one."

"I know." Tori took a second Life Saver. "I know Carla Benson will be there, and I know I can beat her."

"Don't be too confident," Mrs. Carsen warned. "You haven't seen her skate in months. For all you know, she's way ahead of you."

"I'll bet she's not," Tori said. She was just guessing, but she didn't care. Why couldn't her mother encourage her instead of always pointing out how tough things were going to be?

"Anyway, Carla's not the only one you'll have to watch out for," Mrs. Carsen went on. "There's that other girl in Blade Runners, Sharon what's-her-name."

"Sharon Groves?" Tori snorted. "She couldn't even do a double flip the last time I saw her."

"And neither could you," her mother remarked.

Tori sighed and sucked on her Life Savers. Her mother had an answer for everything she said, so why bother saying anything at all?

"I know what you're thinking," Mrs. Carsen began. Tori looked at her, surprised. "You think I never let up. That I never give you any slack. Am I right?"

Tori didn't say anything. Her mother went on.

"There's a reason for that," said Mrs. Carsen. "It's because I love you—and I don't want you to make the same mistakes I made."

"What do you mean, Mom?" Tori asked.

Her mother hesitated, then spoke. "I loved skating when I was young," she said. Tori knew something about her mother's skating career—that she had trained hard but had never made it as far as the Nationals. Her mother had often said that she had started too late and wanted Tori to have the chance she never had—the chance to skate all the way to the top.

"But no one in my family thought it was important," Mrs. Carsen said. "My father—your grandfather—thought it was a waste of time, not to mention money. And my mother thought all I should think about was finding the right man to marry."

Tori saw her mother's lips tighten as she stared out the windshield. Tori looked down at her hands. One thing was for sure—her mother had not found the right man to marry.

"There were times when I didn't feel like working

hard," her mother went on. "And no one made me. No one encouraged me. No one thought it mattered. I can't help thinking that's one reason I never made it as a skater."

Tori listened intently. Her mother had never told her this before. But something didn't make sense.

"I'm glad you're telling me this, Mom," Tori said slowly, "but there's one thing I don't understand. If you were trying to encourage me, why didn't you want me to go to Lake Placid in the first place? Why did I have to convince you?"

Mrs. Carsen's hands tightened on the steering wheel, and a faint blush spread from her neck up to her face.

Was she angry? Tori wondered. Or upset about something? What was bugging her anyway?

"Mom?" she said. "Are you okay?"

"No more questions, Tori," her mother said. "I've told you all you need to know."

3

Half an hour later the Carsens turned off the highway at the exit for Lake Placid, and in a few more minutes they were riding along the town's narrow main street.

"It's so pretty," Tori said, looking at the shops and restaurants. They'd just passed Lake Placid itself, and now they were coming up on Mirror Lake, which ran along one side of Main Street. Mountains from the Adirondack range ringed the small town, their tops dusted with snow. "It's kind of like pictures I've seen of little villages in Switzerland or Germany."

"Mmm," Mrs. Carsen said. "They had the Winter Olympics here in 1932, but the 1980 Olympics really put it on the map. It's turned into a real winter sports capital. Not that you'll be seeing much of it," she added. "This isn't a vacation, you know."

"I know, but we'll have *some* free time," Tori retorted. "Some of those little shops look great."

"First things first," Mrs. Carsen said crisply. "First you win here, Tori. And you won't do that if you don't spend every spare minute working on your programs."

"Okay, okay," Tori said. "I didn't mean I wanted to go shopping all day or anything."

"Good," her mother said. "You're here to work, Tori, remember that."

How could I forget? Tori thought. She's already said it twice in the same breath.

But her mother was right, she had to admit. She was here to work. And win.

Tori's mother had taken a suite at the hotel, two rooms with a fireplace and windows that looked out on Mirror Lake and the Adirondacks beyond. It was big and luxurious, but Tori's mother didn't let Tori waste any time checking it out. She just hurried her out of the hotel and over to the Olympic Center.

The lobby of the center was packed with skaters. Most had skating bags slung over their shoulders and they were wearing warm-up jackets from their own clubs. Tori gazed at all the colors—green and gold, orange and white, neon-pink and silver. She looked for the familiar blue-and-white Silver Blades colors, but she didn't see them. I guess we beat the bus here, she thought.

She *did* see some black-and-red jackets, though. Those were the colors of the Blade Runners. She saw Sharon Groves and Sandy Bower. They both had dark curly hair and were laughing together excitedly. Tori didn't see Carla Benson, but she knew she was here.

"Don't stand there gawking, Tori," her mother said. "Let's take a look at the rink and the locker rooms and get familiar with the place." Leading the way, Mrs. Carsen nudged through the crowd toward one of the doors that opened onto the skating rink.

A blast of cold air hit Tori the moment she stepped inside. Following her mother, she walked down a long ramp with bleachers rising on either side. The ice rink loomed below them.

"It's huge," Tori cried.

"It's no bigger than the rink at home," her mother said. "Both of them are Olympic-size."

"I guess you're right." Tori laughed. "Maybe it just seems bigger because they actually had the Olympics here." And because I'll be competing here, she thought with a nervous shiver.

As they reached the barrier surrounding the rink, Tori found herself standing next to a girl with long, straight blond hair. She was wearing a black-and-red warm-up jacket with the name BLADE RUNNERS on the back. It was Carla Benson.

"Hi, Tori," Carla said. She smiled, but it wasn't a friendly smile.

"Hi." Carla was a lot taller than Tori. Tori hated having to tilt her head up to look at her.

"I was wondering if you'd be here," Carla said. "Last time I saw you skate, you weren't ready for a Regional. Maybe I should congratulate you."

"Thanks," Tori said, in a syrupy-sweet tone. "But you can save the congratulations for the medal ceremony." Smiling back at Carla, Tori turned to her mother. "Come on, Mom, let's go check out the locker room."

Feeling a little better now, Tori led the way back up the ramp.

The ladies' locker room was full of skaters from other clubs. Tori waved to Janet Lake and Kerry Morris, two skaters from New York. They were nice, plus they weren't as good as she was.

Looking around the big room filled with benches and metal lockers, sinks and brightly lit mirrors, Tori frowned. "It's nothing but a locker room," she complained. "We might as well be in Seneca Hills."

Mrs. Carsen scowled at her. "Why should you care about the locker room, Tori? You should be itching to get on that ice and practice.

"We're wasting time here," Mrs. Carsen went on. "Let's see if anyone else has arrived yet. I want to speak to Franz and find out your schedule. You should already be on the ice. You need to work on your jumps and that step sequence. Last time I watched you perform your routine, you looked like a robot. . . ."

Tori gritted her teeth and tried to tune her mother out. Usually Mrs. Carson would be the first to point out that the locker room was crummy. Now she was snapping at Tori for saying it. What was with her? Tori just didn't get it.

As they turned to leave, Tori noticed Carla Benson again. This time she was standing with another girl from her club, and Tori caught them mimicking her mother behind her back.

Oh, no, Tori thought. They must have overheard Mom scolding me. Tori felt her cheeks get hot. Why did her mother always have to embarrass her this way?

But Tori wasn't about to let Carla Benson, her main competition, see that she was ashamed. Instead Tori tossed her head and brushed past Carla and her friend as if nothing had happened.

When Tori and her mother got back to the lobby, she immediately spotted Nikki, Danielle, Jill, and Alex, and hurried over to them. Her mother made a beeline for Mr. Weiler.

"Hey, Tori," Jill said. "Have you seen the rink yet? Isn't it fantastic?"

"It's great," Tori agreed. "How was the bus ride?"

"It was really fun," Danielle said. "We sang and played word games and stuff for a while. But everybody started to get real quiet when we got close to Lake

Placid. I guess we were all going over our routines in our minds."

Tori nodded. She'd done the same thing in the car. Or she'd *tried* to anyway. It wasn't easy to do with her mother lecturing her most of the time. "What's next. Does anybody know?"

"Sure. Mr. Weiler handed out the schedule on the bus," Alex said, pulling a sheet of paper out of his jacket pocket. "Let's see," he said, running a finger down the paper. "All the clubs get some practice time this afternoon and tomorrow. Today—right, here's Silver Blades. You're slotted for three o'clock."

"Well, it's only twelve now," Nikki said. "What do you want to do?"

"We could check out some of those little shops on Main Street," Tori suggested. "Or we could go back to the hotel and hang out." Luckily they were all staying in the same place.

"I don't want to hang out," Jill said. "Especially in the hotel room—it's nice, but it's too small."

"Well, my mom took a suite, and it's really huge," Tori said. "We could order food from room service."

"Room service costs a fortune," Danielle said.

"Yeah, Tori, not everybody can afford suites and stuff like that," Jill reminded her. "Anyway I'm too excited to sit around and eat. Let's walk around the town while we have the chance."

Everyone agreed, and they were moving toward the doors when a tall young woman came up to them. She was about twenty-five, and she was carrying a notepad in one hand and a pen in the other.

"Excuse me," she said. "My name's Barbara Nolan. I'm with the Lake Placid newspaper. You're all here for the Regional competition, I take it."

"Yes," Tori said, feeling a surge of excitement.

"Well, my paper's covering the competition," Ms. Nolan said. "And what I'd like is to follow one of the skaters from the beginning right through the last program. Sort of an insider's view of what one of these things is like. Would any of you be interested?"

Tori was thrilled. What a great break! Being featured in a newspaper story would put her in the spotlight—right where she wanted to be. Carla Benson would just die of envy, she thought as she spotted her rival from Blade Runners across the lobby. Without hesitating, Tori stepped in front of her friends and said, "I'd be very interested."

"Great," Ms. Nolan said. "Let me get your name."

"Tori Carsen," Tori said, spelling it out. "I'm from Seneca Hills, Pennsylvania, and the name of my club is Silver Blades." She turned around so Ms. Nolan could see the name on the back of her jacket. She saw her friends watching her. Jill looked a little stunned.

Maybe Jill wanted to be in the newspaper story, Tori thought with a tiny twinge of guilt. She quickly brushed it aside. She needed this story. It was her big chance to get known. If Jill had wanted to be chosen, she simply should have spoken up faster.

"Okay, and how long have you been skating?" the reporter asked. "Oh, wait. I'm going to need your parents or some adult to sign a release form before we go on with this."

"Oh, that won't be any problem," Tori assured her. Her mom would totally love the publicity. "Here comes my mother now," she added as she saw her mother approaching them.

"There you are, Tori," Mrs. Carsen said, ignoring everybody else, including the reporter. "Now, listen, I have to go back to the hotel. I set up a conference call about the fashion show in half an hour, so I want you—"

"Mom!" Tori interrupted, turning to Ms. Nolan. "This is a reporter from the Lake Placid paper. And she's doing a story on me! All she needs is your permission."

"Tori, there's no time for this," Mrs. Carsen said impatiently, still ignoring the reporter. "There'll be plenty of time for articles when you win. *If* you win, which you won't if you let yourself get distracted so easily. Now come on, we have to go."

Before Tori could say another word, her mother took her arm and pulled her away. Tori glanced back. Jill, Nikki, Danielle, and Barbara Nolan were staring after her in surprise.

What's going on? Tori wondered as she turned back to her mother. This just isn't like Mom.

4

"Tori, you have to concentrate!" Mrs. Carsen called from behind the barrier. "I told you, that step sequence is important!"

Tori groaned silently. It was three-thirty. She'd been working on the elements of her short program, first with Mr. Weiler, and now on her own while Mr. Weiler was coaching somebody else. Mr. Weiler hadn't even asked to see the step sequence. If he wasn't worried about it, why should her mother be?

"Is it the ice?" her mother shouted. "Is it as chopped up as it looks? If it is, I'll speak to—"

"It's not the ice, Mother," Tori interrupted. "Just don't worry—I'll get it right."

"Well, something must be bothering you," her mother insisted.

Tori wanted to tell her mother that *she* was the one who was bothering her. But she clenched her teeth and kept her mouth shut.

"Tori, you're nervous and it's showing," Mrs. Carsen called. "You've got to relax!"

Tori wished she could, but it wasn't easy. She couldn't stop thinking about how she was in Lake Placid, in the very arena where the Olympics had been held not too long before. By this time the day after tomorrow she'd be skating her short program in front of the judges and a huge audience. Tori shivered —she just had to do well.

The short program in competitions was the first part of the event and was worth one third of a skater's total score. It was especially important to do well in the short program because the skaters were ranked by their scores, and that determined the order they'd skate in the last part of the competition, the long program. There were eight elements in the short, or original, program for junior ladies: an axel or a double axel, a double jump, a jump combination, a flying jump spin, a layback spin, a spin combination, a spiral step sequence, and another step sequence that could be straight line, circular, or serpentine. There wasn't much room for choice the way there was in the free skating program, and Tori knew she had to do all the elements and do them right, or the judges would deduct points Not to mention what her own mother's reaction would be.

If only Mom would act like everybody else's parents, Tori fumed. Mrs. Panati was out shopping. Mrs. Wong was here at the rink, but she was filling out postcards and hardly ever glanced up. There were other parents there, but some of them were reading or chatting, and none of them were making remarks about their kids' skating.

Her mother was really driving her crazy, especially since there were so many people at the rink. The members of the other skating clubs, along with their coaches and parents, were hanging around, waiting until the Silver Blades were finished so that they could get on the ice. Tori was extremely conscious of being watched—and judged, even if the other skaters weren't the official judges. Her mother's constant criticisms weren't helping Tori's performance one bit.

"Tori, you don't have much time left," Mrs. Carsen reminded her loudly.

Tori didn't answer. Angrily she swooped around the ice.

Closing her eyes to shut out her mother, Tori visualized her step sequence. Then she launched into this part of her program, performing it perfectly this time.

"Finally," her mother snapped. "I told you you could do it if you just concentrated. Now do it again."

Tori rolled her eyes and glided aimlessly across the ice for a few seconds, her hands on the hips of her bright orange skating dress. She guessed it wouldn't hurt to do the step sequence again. She was just about ready to go into it when Janet Lake and Kerry Morris, whose New York club was also practicing now, skated up to her.

"Hi, Tori. Guess what?" Kerry said. "We think Ludmila Petrova and Simon Wells are here!"

"Really?" Tori glanced around excitedly. Her heart was pounding, and not just from skating. Ludmila Petrova and Simon Wells ran the International Ice Academy, a famous training center in Colorado. They must be scouting for new students. Tori would give just about anything to study with them. "Where? Are you sure?"

"I heard Carla Benson talking in the dressing room," Janet replied. "She said somebody from another club told her they were here. I don't know where that person heard it. Maybe it's just a rumor."

"Wouldn't it be great if they *were* here, though?" Kerry asked. "I mean, just imagine getting picked to train with them!"

If they pick anybody, let it be me, Tori wished.

"Well, anyway, we probably shouldn't even be thinking about them," Janet said. "I'd better get back to work. See you, Tori."

As soon as Janet and Kerry had left, Jill and Danielle skated up. Tori was dying to tell them about the two famous coaches, but before she could say anything, Jill started talking about the rest of the skaters.

"Have you checked out any of the other clubs?" Jill asked. "Some of them are really good."

"They're not that good," Tori said with a toss of her head. "Haven't you been watching those girls from Massachusetts? Kristy Miller broke her ankle last week, and the rest of them are lousy."

"They're hardly lousy," Jill said. "I say we're up against some pretty tough competition, and I haven't even seen Carla Benson skate yet. Have you, Tori?"

"No, and I'm not planning to watch," Tori snapped. "Carla's the biggest snob I've ever met."

Jill burst out laughing. "She is," Tori insisted. "Did I tell you what she said to me when I ran into her before? She said—"

"Tori!" Mrs. Carsen's voice interrupted. "What on earth are you doing? Why aren't you skating?"

"I hate to say it, but she's right," Jill said. "I'd better get back to work too."

Tori skated over to her mother. "Mom, guess what I just heard!" she said. "Ludmila Petrova and Simon Wells are here! You know what that means?"

"It means you'd better keep working, or they won't even give you a second glance," Mrs. Carsen replied. "Honestly, Tori, you can't afford to let something like that enter your mind at all. It'll completely destroy your concentration."

Tori just stared at her mother. Didn't she realize what an opportunity this was? For once Tori found herself wishing that her mother would interfere with her skating.

"Well, well," Mrs. Carsen said suddenly, breaking into Tori's thoughts. "Will you look at that?"

Tori looked around, hoping to see the two famous coaches from Colorado. Instead she saw Carla Benson. The tall blond Blade Runners skater was about ten feet away, behind the barrier. She'd just taken off her warm-up jacket, and Tori realized what her mother was commenting on. Carla looked gorgeous in a silver-colored unitard that shimmered in the light every time she moved.

"She looks absolutely lovely," Mrs. Carsen said.

Tori clenched her teeth. Her mother almost *never* praised other skaters, especially not what they were wearing. Hearing her say something complimentary about anybody was annoying. Hearing it about Carla Benson was infuriating.

"All right, Tori, you've got about ten minutes left," Mrs. Carsen said as she returned to the stands. "Make the most of them."

Too angry to say anything, Tori glided away. How could her mother compliment Carla—but never her own daughter? Didn't she realize how it made Tori feel?

Tori did a few slow turns on the ice, and when she looked back, her mother was gone, and someone else was in her place—the reporter, Barbara Nolan. There was a man standing next to her. He had curly red hair and a camera around his neck.

A photographer, Tori realized. Of course. What would a newspaper article about ice skaters be without pictures?

Tori shot a glance in Carla's direction. Suddenly she

wanted to be in that article more than ever. She felt sure her mother would want her in it too. Maybe Mrs. Carsen had been so worried about that conference call earlier that she hadn't understood who the reporter was. She couldn't possibly make Tori turn down a chance like this.

Tori hurried over to the stands before Ms. Nolan noticed Carla Benson. "Hi," she said, gliding to a stop. "Remember me, Tori Carsen?"

"Sure. Hi, Tori," Ms. Nolan said.

"Listen, I'm sorry about what happened earlier," Tori said. "It was just a misunderstanding. My mother's out getting some tea, but she'll be right back. You can straighten everything out with her then."

Ms. Nolan hesitated. "You do understand, I have to get her permission?"

"Oh, sure!" Tori said.

"While we're waiting, why don't I take your picture?" said the photographer. "That'll save some time."

"Sure, why not?" said Tori. Once her mother realized what publicity this could bring, Tori was positive she wouldn't turn it down.

"All right. Ready, Max?" Ms. Nolan asked the red-haired man.

The photographer nodded, and Tori skated away. Doing backward crossovers, she made a small circle, then stepped with her left foot into the camel spin. As she spun her body around, gaining speed, she lifted her right leg in an arabesque and pulled both her arms back along her body. She could hear the clicking and whirring coming from the photographer's camera as she spun. She hoped Carla Benson was watching. She hoped Ludmila Petrova and Simon Wells were watching too. She'd done the spin perfectly.

"How was it?" she asked, skating back to the barrier.

"Looked good to me," Max said, digging into his camera bag for some more film. "Why don't you skate around for a little while so I can get some more shots?"

But before Tori could move, her mother was suddenly there, her cool blue eyes narrowed in anger.

"This is outrageous!" Mrs. Carsen said, looking furious at Barbara Nolan. "I don't believe I gave you permission to talk to my daughter, and now I find you hounding her. If you don't leave her alone, I'll have you barred from this arena! Come on, Tori. It's time to go. Now."

As Tori hurried off the ice, she saw that Jill and Danielle and the whole Silver Blades club had come off the ice just in time to see her mother embarrass her. Carla Benson had witnessed the whole scene too. As Tori passed the Blade Runners skater, Carla flashed a phony sympathetic smile. Tori had never felt so angry and humiliated in her life.

5

Later, walking with her three friends down Lake Placid's main street, Tori took a deep breath of the chilly air. Thank goodness her mother was back at the hotel, taking frantic phone calls from her assistants. Tori was still so furious about that humiliating scene at the rink, she'd just had to escape.

"Okay, so what are we going to do?" Jill asked, pulling a brochure from her pocket.

The others gathered around and peered over her shoulders. They were standing near the Olympic Speed Skating Oval, a few minutes' walk away from the hotel.

"I wish we could go on the luge or the bobsled," Jill said.

Tori looked at the brochure. The luge and bobsled rides were at the Olympic Sports Complex at Mount

Van Hoevenberg, way to the east of town. "That's miles away," she said, "and it's almost five o'clock. Plus I don't think Kathy would like it much if you risked your neck on the luge, Jill."

"But it looks like so much fun," Jill said. "People do it all the time without getting hurt."

"It doesn't matter anyway," Danielle said, pointing to the brochure. "Look, the luge and bobsled rides don't start for two weeks."

Jill frowned. "I guess it's just as well," she said.

"Let's get something to eat," Nikki suggested.

"I can't!" Danielle wailed. "I've just gotten my weight under control, and I already had a slice of pizza today."

"You can have fruit or something," Nikki said. "Come on, I'm starving."

They wandered back along Main Street, going in and out of some of the souvenir and clothing shops. They passed a newsstand with copies of the Lake Placid newspaper on display. Tori couldn't help noticing that Jill, Nikki, and Danielle exchanged glances when they saw the paper.

Tori's cheeks burned as the embarrassment of the afternoon came flooding back. She knew what they were thinking. She just wished they'd come out and say something. But they didn't.

The four girls were quiet until at last they settled into the booth of a small restaurant.

"Look," Tori said, reaching for a piece of freshly baked bread. "I know what you guys are thinking.

You're dying to talk about that scene my mother made today, so why don't you just go ahead?"

Danielle blushed and took a sip of apple juice. "We didn't talk about it because we figured you were embarrassed, Tori."

"Well, you're right," Tori said. "I was so embarrassed, I wanted to die. And Carla Benson saw the whole thing!"

"Everybody saw the whole thing," Jill remarked.

"Thanks for reminding me," Tori said sarcastically.

"Don't start arguing, okay?" Nikki pleaded.

"I'm not arguing," Tori said. "But you guys are my friends. I don't want you to be afraid to talk to me." Tori sighed and added, "Besides, I need to talk to someone—someone besides my mother."

"Is she all right?" Jill asked.

"Of course she's all right," Tori snapped. She immediately regretted it.

"You don't have to bite my head off," Jill said.

"I'm sorry, Jill," Tori answered.

"I know what Jill means," Danielle spoke up. "Your mother's acting sort of strange."

"This *is* a big competition," said Nikki. "You all seem a little tense to me. Even I feel nervous, and I'm not even skating. Maybe the pressure's getting to your mother too."

Tori shrugged. "You're probably right. But it just doesn't make sense. I really thought my mother would *want* me to be in that article. Especially since Simon Wells and Ludmila Petrova are here."

"What?" Jill squealed. "I didn't know that!"

"How do you know?" asked Danielle.

"I was talking to Kerry Morris and Janet Lake while we were practicing. They told me Petrova and Wells are right here in Lake Placid, looking for skaters to come to Colorado. They've got scouts with them," she added. She wasn't positive about that, but it sounded right.

"Wow," Nikki said softly. "Can you imagine training with them? I wonder if Diana knows."

"Diana?" Tori frowned.

"Well, sure," Nikki said. "I mean, she's in the senior ladies' division—she's practically ready for the Olympics. If they see her, they might want her."

"Maybe," Tori said doubtfully. "But I think they're looking for younger skaters." She wasn't positive about *that*, either, but she didn't like the way Nikki automatically thought of Diana instead of *her*. "Ones who have a lot of potential naturally."

"Naturally," Jill said. "Like one of *us*!"

"Or *all* of us!" said Danielle.

Tori nodded. "Remember when I was doing my camel spin for that photographer? I'm pretty sure I saw one of the scouts watching." It wasn't true, of course, but Tori couldn't resist the chance to impress her friends. "It was before my mother came and messed things up, thank goodness!"

"Well, I hope the scout didn't see *that*," Jill remarked.

"It wouldn't matter," Tori told her. "All that matters is how well somebody skates. They wouldn't care about anybody's mother, not if they think a skater has Olympic potential. And I did that camel spin perfectly. Of course I'll have to do a little bit more than one perfect camel spin," she added with a laugh. "But anyway I'm really excited. If I do a great job in my programs, who knows what might happen?"

"To any of you," Nikki put in. Tori frowned at her.

"Speaking of the programs," Jill said, "I stayed and watched the Blade Runners practice for a few minutes after you left, Tori. Carla Benson's trying a triple toe loop. She landed it every time, and I kept missing mine."

"Practice doesn't count," Nikki reminded her. "I bet when you skate for the judges, you'll land it and she won't."

"I hope so," Jill said nervously. "But she looked great."

"It was that unitard," Danielle said. "It was so beautiful."

Tori was tired of hearing about Carla and her stupid unitard. "I didn't think it was so beautiful," she said. "All that shimmering silver? It made her look like a fish. Anyway," she lied, "my mother said it was made really cheaply. It'll probably fall apart."

"Tori," said Jill, "do you have to listen to *everything* your mother says?"

"I know my mother has her faults," she retorted. "But you don't have to criticize her, Jill."

"Jill wasn't criticizing her," said Danielle. "She was just trying to help you."

"Help?" Now Tori was really angry. "I think you're just jealous, Jill."

"Me?" Jill stared at her friend. "I'm hardly jealous of your mom, Tori," she said softly. "I couldn't stand having her breathing down my neck all the time."

"I mean you're jealous of my outfits," Tori said. "And you're jealous because a scout from Colorado was watching me today, and because I almost got in that newspaper story and you didn't."

"Well, as a matter of fact—" Jill started to say.

"Don't, Jill," Danielle warned.

"Why not?" Jill said. "She's going to find out anyway."

"Find out what?" Tori asked.

"After your mother dragged you away, that reporter talked to me," Jill told her. "She asked me if I'd be interested in being in the article, and I told her yes."

Tori could feel all the color drain from her face. For once she didn't know what to say or do. Now Jill would be the one who'd get all the attention and publicity. She'd be the one everyone was watching.

Why is my mother trying to ruin *everything?* Tori wondered.

6

When Tori opened her eyes the next morning, she couldn't figure out where she was for a moment. The room, the wallpaper, the mattress she was lying on were all unfamiliar.

Then it came back to her. She was in a hotel in Lake Placid. She'd come here yesterday for the Regional figure-skating competition. Tomorrow was the day of the short program.

Tori sat straight up, wide awake now. In the next room she could hear footsteps pacing steadily back and forth. Every few seconds there was the rattling of paper and a low, muttering sound.

Throwing back the blanket, Tori swung her legs to the floor and got out of bed. The only person it could be was her mother, but her mother just wasn't the muttering kind.

But it *was* her mother, Tori discovered as she went quietly into the next room. The low table by the window overlooking Mirror Lake had glasses of juice and two silver-domed plates on it. Mrs. Carsen was clutching a newspaper as she paced the floor, grumbling to herself.

"What's going on?" Tori asked. "What's the matter?"

Mrs. Carsen jumped; she hadn't seen Tori come in. Her face was pale and angry, and she puffed out a big breath of air. "I'm just absolutely furious, that's what's the matter!" she said.

"Well, what is it? Let me see."

Mrs. Carsen glared at the paper one more time, then thrust it at Tori. "Look!"

Tori smoothed it out and looked. There, on the front page, was her photograph. She was doing her camel spin, and the photographer had caught it beautifully. Her leg was in a perfect arabesque, her arms a fluid line along her body, her face turned toward the camera.

Below the photo was a caption that mentioned the competition. Best of all, it gave Tori's name.

"I made it very clear how I felt about publicity," Mrs. Carsen said furiously. "And now I find your photograph in the newspaper. They can't do that without my permission. I should call a lawyer!"

"I never thought they'd use it, not after you said I

couldn't be in the story," Tori said. "I guess it was a mix-up. But isn't it great?" she added excitedly, still looking at the picture. "He caught me at the perfect moment. I knew I looked good, but I didn't know I looked this good!" Carla Benson would be green with envy, she thought happily.

"Some mix-up," her mother retorted. "I specifically told that reporter that you weren't to be a part of this."

"I know." Tori sighed. "I really don't understand what the problem is, Mom," she said. "Kristi Yamaguchi's picture was on the cover of practically every magazine in the country before the 1992 Olympics. It's publicity. You're always telling me publicity's important for my career."

"This is different."

"Why?"

"Because . . . oh, never mind, it just is. Now, why don't you eat something and then take a shower?" Mrs. Carsen quickly changed the subject. "You have a practice session in an hour and another one right after lunch, so we'd better get going."

As Mrs. Carsen went into the bathroom, Tori shook her head. Her mother wasn't making any sense at all.

Tori looked at the photograph again, smiling with satisfaction. If she couldn't be in the article, at least she'd managed to get her picture in the paper. Folding the newspaper, she took it into the bedroom. She wanted the photograph for her scrapbook, even if her mother didn't.

By the afternoon practice session the tension was starting to build. This would be the last real practice before the short program tomorrow. The pairs were skating tomorrow morning, so the singles wouldn't be able to use the ice then. They'd get a few minutes' warm-up before their programs, but that was all.

As Tori skated onto the ice after lunch, she was still feeling pumped up about her photograph. But she felt the tension too. There was a lot more activity around the rink than there had been the day before. Skaters from other clubs were sitting in the bleachers, closely watching the competition. Officials were walking around checking the sound equipment, the lights, and the seating for the judges. Tori wondered if one of the official-looking people was a scout from Colorado.

There wasn't enough time to do all of her original program, so Mr. Weiler had Tori work on three or four elements while he worked with a couple of other skaters.

Tori went over and over her double axel, her double flip jump, and her jump combination, which could consist of either two double jumps or a double and a triple.

Just as she finished a double flip jump, Tori heard

her mother. "Tori!" Mrs. Carsen shouted. "Come over here!"

Gritting her teeth, Tori skated to the edge of the oval.

"You've lost some height on that jump," Mrs. Carsen said. "I don't understand it. How can you do it perfectly at home and not here, where it counts?"

"Mr. Weiler didn't say anything about it," Tori said.

"He doesn't have eyes in the back of his head, Tori," her mother told her. "Franz is watching Danielle right now, so he couldn't see what I saw. Go do it again."

Tori pushed away, skating backward, looking over her shoulder for the spot where she'd plant her toepick and lift off in the double flip.

When she was ready she dug her toepick into the ice, and powered herself high into the air. She pulled her arms in tight to her body, spun two full rotations above the ice, then landed cleanly on one foot, lifting her free leg behind her and her arms out gracefully for balance.

Perfect, she thought.

"It's not there yet!" her mother shouted.

Tori pretended not to hear her. If her mother didn't start leaving her alone, she wouldn't be able to do anything!

Skating toward the other end of the oval, Tori caught sight of Jill trying her triple toe loop. And missing it. As they passed each other, she heard Jill mutter, "I've got to land it, I've got to!"

Tori knew Jill was having trouble, but she couldn't be sympathetic. She was too nervous about her own program, and they were competing against each other. She wouldn't admit it to anyone, but Tori knew she wanted to beat Jill. Besides, she was still annoyed. How could Jill have agreed to do the newspaper story when she knew how much Tori wanted to be in it?

"Hey, Tori," Melinda Daly said as she skated by. "I saw your picture in the paper this morning. You looked great."

"Thanks," Tori said, feeling pleased. Maybe there was a scout watching right now, she thought. If there was, she was sure to be noticed. She was wearing a lemon-yellow skating dress with long, tight sleeves that came to a point on the backs of her hands. The sleeves were sewn with a pattern of small sequins that sparkled when they caught the light. She was the only dressed-up skater; the others were wearing tights and leg warmers, sweatshirts or sweaters.

"Tori, what are you doing?" her mother shouted.

"Getting ready to do my footwork sequence," Tori shouted back.

"All right, but be sure to do the jump again," her mother instructed. "I've set up another conference call, so I have to leave now. I'll see you back at the hotel."

"Thank goodness," Tori muttered as she started on her footwork sequence. Her feet turned and crossed to the beat of the music that was playing in her mind. By now she knew every note of her program music by heart. She coordinated her arm movements with the motions of her feet and worked hard at making the sequence look effortless.

After their practice time was over, Tori, Jill, and Danielle skated off the ice. Nikki and Alex came down from the stands to join them.

"You guys are looking good," Alex said.

"Really great," Nikki agreed.

"Thanks," Jill said. "I hope I look better tomorrow."

Tori unlaced her skates, and when she straightened up, she saw the reporter, Barbara Nolan, walking down the ramp toward the ice.

"Tori!" Barbara called. "I'm glad to see you. I wanted to apologize about that photo of you in today's paper."

"Oh, that's okay—" Tori began.

"No, really," said Barbara. "I know your mother didn't want you to be in the paper, but there was a mix-up and your picture was printed. I'm very sorry."

Before Tori could respond, Carla Benson appeared on the ramp. Barbara waved to her, and Carla waved back.

"There's Carla," she said. "I've got to go. But please give your mother my apologies."

Barbara hurried off to talk to Carla.

Oh, great, Tori thought. First Jill, now Carla.

Suddenly Danielle said, "Tori, there's a guy over there in the stands, and he's looking straight at you!"

7

Startled, Tori looked to where Danielle was pointing and saw a man standing about fifteen feet away
from her.

He had curly blond hair, and he wasn't very tall. He
was too far away for Tori to see the color of his eyes.
But whatever color they were, they were definitely
watching her.

Then, as Tori stared back at him, the man turned
and walked out of the arena.

"You're right," Tori said. "He was looking at me,
Danielle. I wonder who he is."

"Maybe he's a scout!" Nikki said. "Didn't you say
there are scouts around, Tori?"

Jill shrugged. "Maybe he's just watching the skaters," she said. "He doesn't have to have a special reason for watching a warm-up."

"I don't know," said Danielle. "I was watching him for a while, and he seemed interested only in Tori."

"He *must* be a scout!" said Nikki.

Tori's heart began to beat faster. Of course, that had to be it. "I bet that's exactly what he is!" she said. "This is great!" To her satisfaction she saw that the reporter had left, and now Carla Benson was lacing up her skates, close enough to hear everything. "Just think— a scout from a famous training center. I wonder how long he was watching me."

"If he's a scout, he was probably watching everybody," Jill said quickly. "Come on, I want to stop thinking about the competition for a while. Let's get out of here and do something fun."

"Good idea," Danielle said.

"Okay," Tori agreed. She didn't want to stick around and watch Carla Benson skate anyway.

"Don't you have to check with your mother?" Jill asked as they walked out of the arena toward the dressing room.

"She's busy with a conference call," Tori said. "Besides, she doesn't have to know where I am every minute of the day."

"No, just every two minutes," Jill said under her breath.

Tori heard it and shot her a dirty look. She started to say something, but Jill skipped ahead and walked with Nikki.

Forget it, Tori told herself. Jill's just jealous. She's jealous of your skating dresses and your talent and the fact that a scout was watching you, not her.

Thinking about the scout again, Tori grinned to herself. That man had to be from the center in Colorado. Why else would a total stranger be watching her so closely?

To take their minds off the competition, the girls decided to go sledding. As they were leaving the arena, they told Mrs. Wong and Mrs. Panati about their plan for the afternoon.

"Good for you, girls," said Mrs. Wong. "You all could use a break." Mrs. Panati agreed that it was a good idea and promised to let Tori's mother know.

The girls went into town and bought flying saucers in a shop on Main Street, then walked across the street to the snow-covered hill that led down to Mirror Lake. It was a sunny day, and the hill was crowded with sledders shouting happily as they zoomed down toward the lake.

"This looks fantastic!" Jill shouted. Tossing her red flying saucer onto the snow, she jumped onto it and pushed off.

The others jumped onto their own sleds and followed. Tori felt herself relax as her saucer careened down the hill. The wind whipped her cheeks and hair, and the cold air felt great. It was such a relief to be away from the arena and the competition. And it was especially wonderful to be away from her mother.

At the bottom of the slope, her friends were talking to a group of four boys.

"There she is," Danielle said when Tori joined them. "Tori, tell them why we're here. They don't believe us."

"Yeah," one of the boys said with a grin. He was on the short side, slim, with dark curly hair that fell into his eyes. Tori thought he was really cute. "They say you're skating in a competition."

"We are," Jill insisted.

"She's right," Tori said. "Haven't you ever heard of the North Atlantic Regional Competition?" *All* four of the guys were really cute, she decided. The first boy introduced himself. "I'm Jake," he said. "And this is Dave, Mickey, and Tom." Dave was tall with longish blond hair and blue eyes. Mickey had short, straight dark hair and intense dark eyes, and Tom was stocky with light-brown hair and a very cute smile.

"Hey, I think they might be telling the truth," Dave said, staring at Tori. "Didn't I see your picture in today's paper?"

Tori smiled, pleased at being recognized. She'd known something good would come of that photograph—but she hadn't expected this. "That's right," she said. "That was me." All the guys looked impressed, she noticed.

"Well, hey, this is great," Mickey said.

"Yeah," Tom agreed. "Here we are, just four ordinary guys from Lake Placid High, and we run into some celebrities."

Lake Placid *High*? Tori thought in surprise. These guys are in high school—and they're paying attention to *us*!

"We're not exactly celebrities." Danielle laughed.

"No, really, I'm impressed," Jake said. "What are your names? We'll remember to look for you at the next Olympics."

The girls laughed and introduced themselves. Tori could tell that her friends were just as flattered by the older boys' attention as she was.

"So where are you from?" Dave asked.

"Seneca Hills, Pennsylvania," Danielle said.

"I bet you're glad to be out of classes, huh?" Tom asked. "Do you have to study while you're on a trip like this, or does your high school let you off the hook?"

Tori and the others exchanged amazed glances. These guys thought they were in high school!

"Uh, no, we have to study no matter what," Jill said quickly. "Come on," she added, "let's go back up the hill and race down."

"Can you believe it?" Danielle whispered to Tori as they took their sleds to the top of the hill. "They actually think we're in high school!"

"I know," Tori said with a laugh. "But so what? We'll probably never see them again anyway."

"What if they ask us about classes or what colleges we've applied to or stuff like that?"

"Make something up," Tori suggested.

"Right," Danielle agreed, muffling a giggle.

For almost an hour the eight of them stayed together. They raced down the hill on their sleds, two at a time. Jill lost her first race with Tom and started pelting him with snowballs. After that the loser of every race threw snowballs at the winner. Soon they were spending as much time having snowball fights as they did sledding.

Tori's hair was soaking wet and she had snow down the back of her coat, but she didn't care. She was having a ball. Not only were all the guys great-looking but they thought she was really special because her picture had been in the paper. They all wanted to share a sled with her. That's what publicity does for you, she thought happily.

"Okay, okay." The guy named Dave laughed as Jill lobbed another snowball at him. "I surrender."

"It's getting late," Danielle said, looking at her watch. "And tomorrow's the first part of the competition, so we really ought to get back to the hotel."

"So early?" Tom said as they all trudged up the hill together. "We were going to stop somewhere for hot chocolate. It would be great if you guys could come."

"We've all got a big day tomorrow," Tori said. "I wish we could do it again, but—"

"Hey, I've got an idea," Jake interrupted. "You guys said you skate during the day, right?"

"Right," Nikki said.

"So why don't you meet us here tomorrow night?" Jake suggested. "We'll take you tobogganing on Mirror Lake. It's fantastic. Everyone from our school hangs out there."

"Sounds great!" Jill said enthusiastically.

Tori stared at her. Was Jill serious about meeting them when they were in the middle of a big competition? Their parents and coaches would never allow them to meet these boys.

"All right, it's a date," Jake said with a grin. "We'll see you tomorrow night."

Up on Main Street they all said good-bye, and then the four boys went in one direction, the four girls in another.

Nikki burst out laughing. "I cannot believe it!" she said. "I kept wondering when they'd ask me what grade I was in, and I couldn't decide whether to say I was a freshman or a sophomore!"

"Do you think they ever suspected we're only in seventh grade?" Danielle asked.

Jill laughed. "If they did, they didn't seem to care. Anyway that was really fun, wasn't it?"

"Yeah, except you shouldn't have said we'd meet them," Tori told her.

"Oh, come on, Tori," Jill said. "It just popped out.

You know I didn't mean it, and besides, they probably don't really expect us to show up."

"How do you know that?" Tori asked. "They acted like they wanted us to."

"Do you think so?" said Jill. "I figured they were just saying it to be nice. I hope it won't hurt their feelings if we don't meet them."

Tori opened her mouth, but nothing came out. She was looking across the street toward their hotel and saw something that made her forget what she was going to say. She stopped walking so suddenly that Nikki bumped into her from behind.

"Tori!" Nikki said.

"Sorry," Tori murmured. "But look! Right in front of the hotel. Look who's standing there!"

The other three looked. Nikki gasped. "It's that man, Tori! The one who was watching you at the rink earlier."

Tori nodded, keeping her eyes on the man across the street. It was definitely the same one. This proves it, she thought. He's scouting me. "He must have found out my name and where I'm staying and now he wants to talk to me," she said. "He wants me to come train in Colorado. Or maybe some other place. It doesn't have to be Colorado. All the famous training schools probably send scouts."

"So why's he walking away?" Jill asked, pointing.

Tori shrugged. "Maybe he got tired of waiting," she said. "Or maybe he decided he should talk to Mr. Weiler first. That's probably it."

Tori had forgotten all about sledding with the high school boys. This was more important. There were scouts at the competition, and one of them had his eye on her!

8

The next morning when Tori woke up, her heart immediately started to pound. This is the day, she thought.

Today she'd be skating her short program. At the Olympic Arena, in front of the judges. And not only the judges, she remembered. The scout would be there too. She had to be perfect; she just had to!

It was only six o'clock, but Tori was too excited and nervous to try to sleep anymore, or even to stay in bed. She got up and took a shower, mentally running through the elements of her program as she stood under the hot water.

While she was toweling her hair dry, she heard a knock at the door to their room. She came out of the bathroom just in time to see her mother opening an envelope.

"What is it?" Tori asked.

Startled, her mother pulled out a sheet of paper and hastily dropped the envelope into the wastepaper basket. "Nothing, Tori, just something for work." She turned away and opened the sheet of writing paper.

From where she was standing, Tori could see her mother's shoulders tighten as she read the letter. Abruptly she folded the paper and slid it into the pocket of her robe.

"Well!" Mrs. Carsen said brightly, turning to face Tori. "This is the big day, isn't it? You'll have to eat a good breakfast, Tori. I'll take a shower, and we'll go down to the restaurant. Think about your program while you're waiting," she added as she bustled into the bathroom.

Mystified, Tori walked over to the wastepaper basket and fished around for the envelope. She knew the letter had been for her mother. She knew she shouldn't be poking into her business, but she couldn't help being curious. Her mother had acted almost guilty, as if she was trying to hide something, and Tori wanted to know what it was.

Dragging the crumpled envelope out, Tori smoothed it in her hands and turned it over. But the letter, whatever it was about, hadn't been for her mother at all.

Printed neatly and clearly in the center of the envelope were the words *Miss Tori Carsen*.

It was for me, Tori thought, amazed. But why wouldn't Mom let me see it?

She sat at the desk for a moment, stunned. Her mother had been acting strange lately, but this was the strangest thing of all. She had never known her mother to be so mysterious with her. Was she hiding something?

Tori dropped the envelope back in the basket and tried to calm herself down. It's the competition, she told herself. That must be it. Whatever this is about, Mom doesn't want to bring it up during the competition. She's probably afraid I'll lose my concentration. But what could shake me up that much?

An answer immediately popped into Tori's mind. The scout.

Of course, Tori thought. The letter must have been from the scout. Mom knows I'm excited about that— and she doesn't want it to distract me.

But the more she thought about it, the more excited she became.

The ladies' locker room was quiet later that day, but it wasn't a calm kind of quiet. The girls didn't talk much, and when they did, they talked softly. But every once in a while a nervous laugh would erupt, and it sounded like a crack of thunder right before a storm.

Checking the big clock on the tiled wall, Tori saw

that she had about half an hour before she went on. Jill would go first.

Carla Benson and another skater from Blade Runners went next, and then it would be Danielle's turn. There'd be a break, and then Tori would be on.

Five minutes at the most for warm-up, Mr. Weiler had told her. Just get the heart pumping and the blood going, but don't go overboard. Tori did a few leg stretches and knee bends, wondering if it was possible for her heart to pump any faster than it already was.

Stopping her stretches, Tori turned to Danielle and Jill, and to Nikki, who was there to wish them luck. "Guess what?" she said. "My mother got a note from that scout."

"Really? What did it say?" Nikki asked.

"Well, I didn't actually read it," Tori said. "I think my mother's saving it for a surprise. But it probably told her he was interested in having me come to train in Colorado. I mean, what else could it have said?"

Out of the corner of her eye Tori saw Carla Benson. The tall blond Blade Runners skater was pretending to do some leg stretches. But Tori could tell she was listening to every word.

Raising her voice a little, Tori said, "I can't wait to talk to him. I wonder if I'll be finishing out the year in Seneca Hills or if he'll want me to come to Colorado right away."

"According to you, there are scouts from all over the world," Jill said. "Maybe he'll want you to go train in Timbuktu."

Carla Benson giggled softly.

"Listen, you guys, could you keep it down, please?" Sandy Bower asked. "I'm trying to concentrate."

"I don't know for sure that he's from Colorado," Tori whispered to Jill. "But I do know he's a scout and he's interested in me. You might be glad for me instead of acting so snotty about it."

"Come on," Danielle pleaded. "Sandy's right. Everybody's trying to concentrate."

For a few minutes no one said anything. Tori did some more knee bends, thinking about her program. And about the scout.

She watched as Mrs. Wong started helping Jill into her skating dress. It was red of course, with wide bands of silver ribbon at the neck and hem. It was a little flashy, Tori thought. Jill would look great in a simple emerald green, but she was too stubborn to listen to any advice from Tori.

"You look great, Jill," Nikki said.

"Thanks," Jill said nervously. "How's my hair? The ribbon's not loose, is it?"

"What ribbon?" Tori asked. "All I see is a rubber band."

Jill reached up and felt the end of her braid. "What happened to it? I know I put a ribbon on."

Mrs. Wong, Nikki, and Danielle searched the floor.

"What color was it?" Nikki asked.

"Red, what else?" Tori couldn't help saying.

"Do you mind, Tori?" Jill snapped.

Tori shrugged.

"Please, everybody's nervous," Mrs. Wong said. "Snapping at each other will just make it worse." She stopped looking around the floor. "Well, it doesn't matter, Jill. You look fine without one."

"Wait a sec," Nikki said, reaching up to her hair. "You can borrow mine if you want." She untied her hair ribbon and handed it to Jill.

"Thanks, Nikki." Jill took the ribbon and tied it around her braid. "How does it look?"

Ugh, Tori thought. It clashed with Jill's red dress, but she decided not to say anything else. Jill could figure that out for herself if she wanted to.

"Well, it's better than nothing," Jill said. She marched out of the locker room. Nikki hurried out to go to her seat and watch. "Good luck, everybody," she said as she went out the door. "I know you'll all be great. Go, Silver Blades!"

As soon as Jill and Nikki left, Mrs. Carsen swept into the locker room. "Tori, don't just stand there; you should be warming up," she said. "Don't let your muscles get cold."

Tori went back to her knee bends. For a few minutes, she fumed about Jill. Despite the fact that they had been bickering the whole trip, Jill was one of her best friends. So why hadn't she taken Tori seriously when Tori mentioned the scout? It was almost as if Jill didn't believe her.

Put it out of your mind, Tori told herself. It's time to

concentrate on your skating.

Carla Benson left for the ice, and Danielle followed a few minutes later. Tori wished her friend luck, then pulled on her ice-blue skating dress and sat to lace up her skates. Every movement was automatic. Mentally she was going through the elements of her original program. Her mother was still here, and Tori wished she'd leave, so she could have the last few minutes alone. But at least her mother knew enough to keep quiet.

Finally it was time. Tori and her mother left the locker room together. Tori would have a couple of minutes on the ice with four or five other skaters, a last warm-up, and then she'd be the first of that group to go on.

Mrs. Carsen gave her a quick hug and went to find her seat in the bleachers. As Tori walked along the ramp down to the waiting area, she heard a big cheer and even some whistling.

Just before Tori reached the waiting area, she saw Danielle coming toward her. Her big brown eyes were sparkling, and she gave Tori a thumbs-up signal. "I did pretty well," she said quickly. "And Jill did too. Triple and everything!" She reached out and squeezed Tori's arm. "Good luck!"

Tori smiled and said, "Congratulations." Then she moved past her friend and on down to the ice. It was *her* turn now.

On the ice for a quick warm-up with the other skaters, Tori did a couple of spins and jumps. She also did backward crossovers and part of her step sequences. She didn't push herself; she didn't try to give it everything. This was just to loosen up, to get the feel of the ice again. Because she was the first skater to perform after the break, Tori left the ice a minute before the other girls.

The warm-up time was over. The rink was empty. Tori waited behind the barrier, still going through the moves in her mind. She could hear shuffling and chattering in the stands and the voices of other coaches giving their skaters last-minute instructions. It was background noise and it wasn't quiet, but Tori was too focused to let it distract her.

Then an official gave her the signal. Tori took a deep breath and started onto the ice. Mr. Weiler had told her to pin her eyes to the center of the rink, where she'd get into position for the start of her program. Tori was never sure why she did it, but at the last second she glanced at the bleachers to her right.

There he was! The man who'd been watching her, the one who'd sent a note to her mother. The scout from Colorado was in the first row, and he was looking straight at her!

Startled, Tori jerked her head and looked away from the scout. But it was too late. She felt her balance going, and before she could stop it from happening, she glided toward the center of the rink—on her backside!

9

A cry of surprise went through the audience as Tori slid across the ice. Tori thought she heard laughter too.

Tori took only seconds to scramble to her feet, but it felt like hours. How could I? she thought miserably. How could I have fallen before I even started? This is the most embarrassing thing I've ever done! Her mother was going to have a fit. And the scout—what would he think?

Tori somehow managed to skate into position in the center of the ice. The judges won't begin evaluating you until the music starts, she told herself. The fall won't hurt your score.

Tori brushed the ice from her dress and tights and then raised her arms and chin. As she waited for the

music to start, she put a smile on her face. She was
faking it, but she knew nobody could tell. She was
used to covering up with a smile every time her mother embarrassed her, and by now the smile could fool
anybody.

Then the music came, an instrumental medley from
the Broadway show *Les Misérables*, and on the fourth
beat Tori started her program. She skated in a wide
circle, then came back toward the center of the rink
using her spiral step sequence. As she went into a
double toe loop, she knew she hadn't gotten as much
height as she wanted. She just barely managed to get
both rotations in before landing. At least she stayed on
her feet and came out of the jump without a wobble.
She'd done it.

It's going to be all right, Tori told herself, and as
she heard the clapping from the audience, her spirits
started to climb. She was going to be better than all
right; from now on she'd be flawless.

Skating backward crossovers clockwise around the
side of the rink, Tori prepared to do her double Lutz.
She relaxed her arms and looked over her right shoulder. Then, as she reached back with her right leg and
arm for the takeoff, she looked forward. She placed
her right toepick on the ice and sprung from her left
leg, bringing her left arm and shoulder back and her
right arm and shoulder forward. Once in the air, she
pulled her arms and legs into rotating position, spun
counterclockwise once, and landed on her right foot.

The applause was louder this time. Now they weren't

clapping because they felt sorry for her, Tori thought. They were clapping because they were impressed.

The rest of the three-and-a-half-minute program went almost perfectly, and when Tori spun to a stop in the center of the rink, her smile was firm and sure. Anyone looking at her would find it hard to believe that she'd started out with a fall.

I made it through, Tori thought, and she couldn't help feeling proud of herself in spite of her fall. What she had just done took courage, and she knew it.

The locker room was a madhouse. There were still other skaters out on the ice, but everyone from Silver Blades had finished their programs, so most of them were in the locker room, along with skaters from New Hampshire, New Jersey, Massachusetts, Rhode Island, and of course Vermont's Blade Runners.

As Tori changed out of her skating dress, she listened to everybody discussing their scores.

"A four-point-oh on technical," Sandy Bower from the Blade Runners wailed. "I can't stand it."

"Yeah, but you got four-point-fives and four-point-sixes on artistic," her friend Sharon Groves said.

Nine judges awarded two marks, from 0.0 to 6.0. One mark was for technical merit, or how well each element was performed. The second was for artistic impression, or how well a skater had performed to the music. After all the scores had been added up, the skaters would be ranked in order for the long program. The scores for the short program counted for one third of the total score for the competition.

"I haven't got a chance at a medal," Tori heard Sandy say. "There are twelve skaters ahead of me."

Tori knew she was one of those twelve skaters ahead of Sandy Bower. But she had no reason to celebrate. After she looked at the standings, she forgot how proud she'd felt at the end of her program. Carla Benson, with scores from 5.3 through 5.8, was in first place, and Jill, whose scores ranged from 5.2 to 5.6, was in second. Tori, scoring 5.2s and 5.3s, was third in the standings. Third. That wasn't good enough. Tomorrow she would have to skate better than she'd ever skated. Because she couldn't be third. She had to win.

"Hey, Tori, congratulations," Danielle said, pulling a yellow turtleneck over her head. "Third place isn't bad." Danielle was in sixth place, behind Janet Lake.

"Thanks," Tori said.

"And Jill's in second," Nikki said. "That gives Silver Blades a chance to bring home a medal. Isn't that great?"

"I couldn't believe I actually landed my triple," Jill said, brushing her hair. "I was so worried about it, I almost decided to do a double instead, but at the last minute I went for it."

Tori closed her eyes. She knew she should be happy

for Jill, and maybe she would be if the circumstances were different. But this competition was important to Tori's career. She really wanted to win. She opened her eyes and reached for a blue wool sweater. She noticed Carla Benson watching her.

"Well, Tori," Carla said, "I guess I should congratulate you. You're actually in third place. It's amazing, after that fall you took."

"I'm sure it is amazing to you, Carla," Tori said. "If you'd fallen, you'd probably be in last place."

Carla clicked her tongue and turned away.

"What happened, anyway?" Danielle asked Tori. "One minute you were standing and the next you were sliding."

"Thanks for reminding me," Tori snapped. "A fall like that could happen to anyone, you know. Anyway," she added, wanting to change the subject, "guess who was watching me perform? That scout, the one who's been watching me ever since we got here! I may be in third place now, but my long program is going to be absolutely perfect. I just know he's going to want me in Colorado!"

Before anyone could respond, there was a flurry of activity at the door, and then Tori heard her mother's voice. "Excuse me!" Mrs. Carsen said loudly. "I have been trying to get in here for the past fifteen minutes! Excuse me!"

Excusing herself all the way across the locker room, Mrs. Carsen finally stopped in front of Tori.

"Tori, I was absolutely shocked," she said. "You recovered well from that horrendous fall, but what happened?"

Tori wished she could drop through the floor. Everyone could hear her mother scolding her.

"Third place," Mrs. Carsen went on, her voice boomeranging around the tiled room. "Not bad, but you've got your work cut out for you. I told you how important concentration is. I simply couldn't believe you lost it."

Tori felt a hot blush of anger and embarrassment flood her face, but she didn't say anything.

"Hurry and finish dressing, Tori," her mother instructed. "Then we'll go talk to Franz. Maybe he can get you some extra practice time before the long program."

As Mrs. Carsen pushed her way back out of the room, Tori picked up a brush and started rapidly pulling it through her hair.

"I can't believe it," Jill said to Tori. "You're actually hurrying."

"What do you mean?"

"I mean, how long are you going to let your mother push you around?" Jill asked. "She came in here and totally humiliated you and you didn't even bother to stand up for yourself. And now you're hurrying to go talk to Mr. Weiler, just like your mother told you."

"That's not true!" Tori said hotly. "I'm just getting ready."

Jill shook her head. "What if your mom tells you

you can't go train in Colorado? Will you argue with her? Ha!"

"She wouldn't do that!" Tori said. "Anyway you're just jealous because a scout's been watching *me*, not you! That's why you're acting like this."

"I am not jealous," Jill said through gritted teeth. "I'm only trying to help you. You'd have a lot more energy to focus on your skating if you didn't have to deal with your mother all the time. You're thirteen years old, but you let your mother control everything you do! Why don't you stop being such a wimp?"

"Wimp, huh?" Tori said angrily. "Let's see who's a wimp. I plan to go meet those high school boys tonight. What about you, Jill? Are you going? After all, you're the one who told them we'd show up!"

Jill barely hesitated. "Sure, I'm going. We're all going, right, guys?" she added, glancing at Nikki and Danielle, who looked surprised.

Tori had surprised herself. Before this minute she had had no intention of meeting those guys, and she'd hardly expected Jill to say she was going too. But Jill had taken the dare.

Well, if Jill's going, *I'm* going, Tori told herself. She wasn't going to let Jill call her a wimp again.

Mrs. Carsen poked her head in the door. "Tori! What are you doing in there? I told you to hurry up!"

Furious at both her mother and Jill, Tori spun around and shouted, "I'll be out when I'm ready, Mother! Just stop ordering me around!"

10

In the hotel suite that night Tori came out of the shower and found her mother reading quietly in one of the armchairs. It was a strange sight. Usually Mrs. Carsen would start talking about skating the minute Tori entered the room. But now she was silent.

Tori knew her mother was angry about the way Tori had yelled at her earlier. Tori hadn't really meant to yell; she was just so furious with Jill and everything, she hadn't been able to stop herself.

But she wasn't about to apologize either. Tori knew Jill was right. Her mother pushed and criticized and yelled all the time, and Tori was sick of it.

Suddenly Mrs. Carsen snapped the book shut and yawned. "I'm going to make a few phone calls and then I think I'll go to bed," she said, getting up.

"Fine," Tori said.

"See you in the morning." Hardly glancing at Tori, she went into the bedroom and shut the door.

Tori took a deep breath and let it out. It felt funny, not having her mother tell her she should go to bed too. But she guessed she was lucky. After all, she'd challenged Jill to go to Mirror Lake to meet those boys, and she would never have managed to get away if her mother had been acting normal.

It was only eight-thirty. Her mother was furious, Tori decided with a grim smile. She never went to bed that early.

Sitting in the chair, Tori leafed through a magazine for fifteen minutes. Then she got up and tiptoed to the bedroom door. She leaned against it and listened. She couldn't hear a sound.

Tori tiptoed away and put on her parka. She checked the pockets to make sure she had money and her room key, then quietly let herself out of the suite.

In the hall she waited a few seconds, her heart pounding. But no sound came from inside the suite. A little scared, but mostly excited, Tori ran down the hall and got into a waiting elevator.

Jill, Nikki, and Danielle were already in the lobby. They'd all managed to sneak away, and they looked as excited as Tori.

Jill smiled at Tori. "You showed up," she said.

"I told you I would, didn't I?" Tori said. "Come on, let's get out of here and have some fun."

"Do you think they'll be there?" Nikki asked as the four friends hurried across the street toward Mirror Lake.

"I don't know," Jill said. "I'm not worried about that, though. I'm more worried about what my mother'll say if she finds out about this."

Tori was worried about the same thing, but she wasn't willing to admit it.

"I don't think this is such a good idea," Danielle said. "I mean, going out on the night before a competition . . ." Her voice trailed off as if she was so amazed at what she was doing, she could barely finish her sentence. "And tobogganing. What if one of us twists an ankle or something?"

"Stop worrying, Danielle," said Jill. "We're all tense. We need to blow off a little steam."

"Besides," said Nikki, "I bet they won't be there."

"If they're not there, then we'll just go tobogganing by ourselves," Tori said. "We don't need them."

But the boys were at the lake, just as they'd said they'd be. Jill spotted them first and waved. "Hey!" she cried. "We're here!"

The guys were happy to see them. "I wasn't sure you'd come," Jake said.

"We said we would," Tori told him. "Right, Jill?"

"Right." Jill grinned. "We wouldn't have missed it. Come on, let's ride!"

They piled into the toboggans, pushed them off, and sped down the hill onto frozen Mirror Lake. Once on the ice, the toboggans kept gliding, and when they slowed down, one of the riders would get out and push, then hop back in.

Speeding across the ice at night was exhilarating. And the boys were just as nice as before. Tori kept glancing at Tom—and he was usually looking at her. She couldn't believe he was in high school—and so cute. For a while Tori forgot about her fall and her fight with her mother and Jill.

"Hey, how did it go today?" Mickey asked the girls as they pulled the toboggans back up the hill. "Did anyone win a medal?"

"We don't know yet," Danielle told him. "We have to skate a second time."

"But I'm in third place right now," Tori said.

"Third?" Tom raised his eyebrows and whistled. "I'm impressed."

"Jill's in second," Nikki said.

Tori scowled at her. "Hey, we didn't come here to talk about the competition, right? Let's sled some more."

Tom didn't seem to care that Jill was ahead of Tori in the competition—he stayed near Tori the rest of the evening.

Once, after the tobaggan had run to the other side of the lake and stopped, Tori stood up and looked at the sky. It was a crystal-clear night, and the starlight sparkled in the sharp air.

"I think it's so cool, what you guys are doing," Tom said.

Tori looked up at him. "You mean skating?"

Tom nodded. "Sure. I mean, it must be a lot of hard work, but it makes you different from most girls. You know—special."

Wow, Tori thought. This guy is really nice. If only he lived in Seneca Hills.

But before she had a chance to say anything, *splat!* a snowball hit Tom in the arm. A second one whizzed past Tori, just missing her back.

"Hey! Who threw that?" she yelled. She turned around and saw Jill and Mickey stooping in the snow, packing more snowballs.

"Are we going to let them get away with that?" asked Tom.

"No way," Tori said, smiling at him. They quickly bent down and scooped up some snow. Nikki, Danielle, and the other boys joined in, and soon there was a full-fledged battle on the ice.

Finally it was ten o'clock. "I think we'd better call it quits," Danielle said.

"Okay," Jake agreed. "Who's for pizza?"

Tori was starting to get worried again. What would happen when she got back? If her mother had woken up and found her gone, she'd probably have the police out looking for her. But Tori didn't want to say no to the guys, not in front of Jill, so she was relieved when Danielle said it.

"We've really got to get back to the hotel," Danielle said. "We skate our long programs tomorrow afternoon, and our coaches would just about kill us if they found out we'd been out late."

Nikki and Jill agreed. Tori noticed that Jill looked relieved too. So much for not being a wimp, she thought.

"Well, okay," Tom said, looking disappointed. "Anyway, we're glad you came."

"Me, too," Tori said. "It was great!"

"Yeah, thanks for asking us," Jill said.

"If you ever come back to Lake Placid, be sure to look us up," said Jake.

"And good luck in the competition tomorrow," said Dave.

"Hey!" said Tori. "Why don't you come to the arena and watch us tomorrow?"

"We'd love to," said Tom. "But some of us have to go to school tomorrow—unlike some celebrities we know."

The girls laughed and started back to the hotel, waving good-bye.

As they hurried through the lobby a few minutes later, Tori felt a knot of dread in her stomach. If her mother was awake and caught her coming in at this hour . . . She could tell her friends were anxious too. No one was saying a word.

Nikki, Danielle, and Jill got off the elevator at the third floor. Tori whispered good-night to them, then rode up alone to her suite at the top.

Outside the suite she held her breath, then inserted the key as quietly as possible. She pushed open the door and listened. Not a sound, thank goodness. All she had to do now was undress and get into bed and her mother would never know a thing.

Holding her breath again, Tori opened the bedroom door. The room was shadowy, but not completely dark because of the moonlight coming in the window. Tori glanced at her mother's bed, half expecting Mrs. Carsen to leap out and start screaming at her.

But the bed was empty.

Tori pushed the door open all the way and turned on the light. The room was empty. She went out and checked the bathroom. Empty. Where was her mother?

Afraid Mrs. Carsen might really have called the police, Tori left the suite and rode down to the lobby. Surely her mother would have notified the hotel management if she thought Tori was missing.

As Tori hurried toward the main desk, she glanced into the coffee shop. She froze in her tracks.

Her mother was inside the shop having a cup of coffee. And she wasn't alone. Sitting across the table from her was the scout from Colorado!

11

Tori backed away from the door of the coffee shop, a big grin on her face. Finally the scout had made contact with her mother! They were probably discussing Tori right this very minute!

For a moment Tori thought about going into the shop and joining them. She was dying to hear what the scout had to say about her. But she decided not to. She might ruin some tricky negotiation or something.

Tori absolutely had to talk to someone, though. She went back to the elevator and rode up to the third floor, then hurried down the hall to her friends' room. They were all sharing one, and Jill's and Danielle's mothers shared another.

She knocked softly and waited. "Who is it?" Nikki's voice asked.

"It's me. Tori!"

Nikki pulled open the door, and Tori went inside. Danielle and Jill, already in their nightshirts, were sitting on one of the beds, playing cards. "What happened?" Nikki asked. "Did you get caught coming in?"

Tori shook her head. "No, but something happened," she said excitedly. "My mom wasn't there when I got back, so I went down to the lobby and saw her in the coffee shop. She was sitting at a table with that scout!"

Wading through a pile of duffel bags and suitcases, Tori plopped down on one of the other beds. "I just know they're talking about me going to train in Colorado! This is the most exciting thing that's ever happened to me in my life!"

"So why aren't you there?" Jill asked, playing another card.

"I thought about going in, but I didn't want to mess anything up," Tori said.

"What do you mean?" Nikki asked, sitting next to Tori.

"I don't really know." Tori laughed. "When it comes to contracts and stuff, my mother knows a lot more than I do, so I'll let her do the talking."

"As usual," Jill muttered.

"Jill," Danielle said in a warning tone.

"No, let her say what she wants to," Tori said. "I can take it. I'm just surprised that one of my closest friends is acting like this when something totally wonderful is happening to me."

"I don't see how you can be sure that it *is* happening yet," Jill said. "But if it is, I can't believe you'd let your mother work everything out behind your back."

"She's not doing it behind my back," Tori argued.

"Oh, yeah? What do you call what's happening?" Jill asked.

"She's not doing it behind my back," Tori said again. "This is just the first stage probably."

"Well, if it were *my* life, I'd want to be in on the first stage." Jill tossed her cards on the bed. "Why are you letting her run things?"

"My mother'll work out the best deal possible for me," Tori said.

"Oh, so suddenly you're not mad at her anymore?" Jill asked.

"The only reason I yelled at her was because of you," Tori said, her voice rising. "If it hadn't been for you, nothing would be wrong!"

"Oh, come on!" Jill's voice rose too. "Yelling at your mother was the first sign of guts you've shown. Why don't you march down to the coffee shop and tell her to stop running your life?"

"And why don't *you* just stay *out* of my life!" Tori shouted. Furious, she turned and ran out of the room.

Up in the suite Tori kicked off her boots, too angry to care if they hit and broke anything. What was happening? How could Jill have said those things to her?

I thought she was my friend, Tori thought. But all she does is criticize me. She's getting as bad as my mother!

As for her mother, Tori was still mad at her too. Tori *should* be included in the talks with the scout. It *was* her life. If she hadn't been so mad, she would have gone down to the coffee shop right then and there. But she'd probably start yelling the minute she saw her mother's face.

Jill was right, Tori thought, but that only made her feel more angry. She didn't want Jill to be right.

Tori stomped into the bedroom, threw off her clothes, and got into bed. All she wanted to do right now was to shut out the entire world. She yanked the blanket over her head and waited for sleep.

At breakfast in the coffee shop the next morning, there was an uneasy silence. Tori waited anxiously to see if her mother would say anything about her sneaking out, but Mrs. Carsen didn't say a word about it. Tori couldn't believe it.

But even more puzzling was Mrs. Carsen's silence about the scout.

Just what is going through her mother's mind? Tori wondered. Lately Tori couldn't predict what her mother would do.

Finally, Tori couldn't stand it anymore. Pushing her

plate of toast aside, she leaned her elbows on the table and said, "I want to talk."

"I have just one request," said Mrs. Carsen, softening a little. "Whatever happens today, I hope you won't scream at me the way you did yesterday—ever again. I was absolutely humiliated."

This was not what Tori wanted to talk about, but she decided to go ahead and get it out of the way. "So was I," she said. "You came in and embarrassed me in front of everybody by making a big deal about my fall. And you're always doing stuff like that. You make comments and yell all the time. You never leave me alone, never. And you're always comparing me to other skaters, telling me I'd better work harder or they'll beat me."

"Tori, I just want you to be the best you can be," Mrs. Carsen said.

"No, you don't," Tori said. "You want me to be the best, period."

Mrs. Carsen started to say something, but just then the waiter arrived with the coffeepot. Tori waited until he'd poured her mother's coffee and left. Then she said, "And there's something else. Remember when I told you about Ludmila Petrova and Simon Wells being here? Well, I don't know if *they're* actually here, but I've seen a man watching me and I'm almost positive he's a scout. And last night proved it."

Mrs. Carsen frowned. "What do you mean, 'last night'? What happened last night?"

"I saw you," Tori said accusingly. "I saw you with him in the coffee shop, talking. And that letter you got," she went on. "I found the envelope you threw away, and I saw it was addressed to me. The scout wanted to talk to me, and you didn't even tell me about it. And you still haven't told me about it!"

Mrs. Carsen looked completely shocked. She was silent for a moment. Then she took a deep breath. "Well," she said. "I suppose I knew all along I'd have to tell you. I didn't want to. I still don't want to."

"Tell me what?" Tori asked impatiently.

"The man you've been talking about lives here, in Lake Placid," Mrs. Carsen said. "When he saw your name and photograph in the paper, he came to the rink to see you. Then he tried to write you a note, but I didn't want you to see it."

"Why not?" Tori asked. "How could you decide that? Who is he?"

Mrs. Carsen sat up straighter and looked Tori in the eyes. "He's not a scout, Tori," she said. "He's your father."

12

At first Tori wasn't sure she'd heard right. "He's what?"

"Your father," Mrs. Carsen said again. She folded her hands on the table and stared at Tori.

Tori stared back. Her face felt hot and prickly, and her heart was racing. She knew she'd heard right the first time, but she still couldn't believe it. "My father?" The words came out in a croak.

Her mother nodded. "When he left us—you were just six months old—I didn't know where he had gone. He left for Europe, to become a ski instructor in the Alps, it turned out. He didn't even have the decency to tell me where he went or why he left. He wrote to me when he moved back to the States two years ago," she said. "And then he tried to send me child support."

"Money?" Tori asked.

"Yes." Her mother raised her chin. "But I didn't take it. I'd built up my business by then and I didn't want his money. I sent every check back and told him to stop writing."

Tori's mind was a jumble of questions; she couldn't even think what to ask first. Her father! No wonder he'd looked at her so closely—he must have known exactly who she was. He'd read about her in the paper and come to the arena. But why hadn't he said anything to her? "He probably thought I wouldn't believe him," she said out loud.

Her mother frowned. "What?"

Tori's voice still sounded funny, and she cleared her throat. "I was thinking," she explained, "about why he never said anything to me."

Mrs. Carsen sniffed. "He didn't say anything because I warned him not to," she said. "Even after I sent his checks back, he kept writing, wanting to know how you were, what you were doing, if you were happy. Imagine him thinking he had a right to know about the daughter he'd left!"

The thoughts and questions were still whirling around in Tori's mind, but a few things were starting to make sense. Now she knew why her mother hadn't wanted to come to Lake Placid at first—it was because her father was here.

"He wanted to meet me after he saw my picture, didn't he?" Tori said. "And you told him no."

"That's right," her mother said. "I told him no."

"You didn't even ask me!" Tori exclaimed. "See? You're always trying to run things for me." She picked up her orange juice, just holding it in her hands. "But this is even worse, Mom—you've been lying to me all this time. About my own father."

"Maybe so, but I did it for a good reason." Pushing her coffee cup aside, Mrs. Carsen leaned forward and put her elbows on the table, something she was always telling Tori not to do. "All the things you say I've done that bother you so much, I've done because I thought they were best. And I don't see that any good could come out of a meeting with your father. He left you, remember? He doesn't deserve to get to know you, and certainly not right in the middle of a competition! You'd be upset and distracted and—"

"I'm already upset and distracted!" Tori knew she was yelling, but she didn't care. "You're always making decisions for me, telling me what to do! You wouldn't even let me decide whether to see my own father. You can't run my life, Mother!"

Tori set her glass down and took a deep breath. "I want to meet him," she said.

An hour later Tori was waiting alone, downstairs in the lobby. Her father was on his way and her mother had agreed to stay upstairs until Tori returned. At least Mom won't be interfering today, Tori thought, sighing.

Now that her father was coming, she was having second thoughts. Tori was too nervous, and not just about him. This afternoon she'd be skating her long program. She should be going over that program, not worrying about some man she'd never met. This was probably a stupid thing to be doing now. Maybe she should just forget the whole thing.

"Tori?" a voice said behind her.

Tori jumped and turned around. There he was. The man she'd been seeing for days and assumed was a scout. She felt a blush wash over her. Talk about jumping to conclusions.

"Hi," Tori said softly.

Mr. Carsen glanced around the lobby. "It's nice outside," he said. "Do you want to take a walk?"

"Sure." Tori didn't care. She didn't know what to say, so it didn't matter where they were.

Outside, the sun was blindingly bright. Tori squinted at her father out of the corner of her eye as they walked down to Mirror Lake. Now that he was up close, she could see that she resembled him. He was short like her and he had light curly hair. It felt so strange—was this man really her father?

Mr. Carsen broke the silence first. Staring at the lake, he cleared his throat nervously, and said, "You skated well yesterday, Tori. You must be happy."

"Not really," Tori said. "I'm in third place. If I hadn't fallen, I might be in second, maybe even first."

"Well, you have another chance, right?" Mr. Carsen said.

Tori nodded. Words were sticking in her throat. What did she have to say to this man who had walked out on her and her mother so long ago? Where had he been all these years?

"Do you ski?" her father asked.

"Some," Tori said. "Is that what you are still—a ski instructor?"

He shook his head. "I'm in architecture now. I still ski, but I gave up teaching when I came back from the Alps."

The Alps, Tori remembered. That's where he'd gone when he'd left her. "How could you?" she blurted out. "How could you have walked out on us like that?"

Mr. Carsen looked uncomfortable. "I was young," he said. "I know that's no excuse, but—"

"It sure isn't," Tori snapped. "Adults are always telling kids to learn responsibility, and then they do things like you did—walk out on them."

"Please, Tori," her father said. "I didn't want to meet you so we could argue."

"Then why did you want to meet me?" Tori asked. "Why'd you wait so long? And you still haven't told me why you left in the first place."

"There's not a simple explanation," Mr. Carsen said.

"Look, I can tell you're upset, and I'm sorry. I don't want it to be this way."

"You're right, I am upset," Tori said. "Wouldn't you be? And how did you expect it to be? Did you think I'd give you a big hug or something?" Her voice cracked. "It's really hard for me, you know. Mom's always on my case, and I never get a break . . ." Tears filled her eyes.

Her father stared at her helplessly. He didn't seem to know what to do.

Finally he put a hand on her shoulder. "I'm sorry, Tori," he mumbled softly.

"Listen, I know you must be nervous about skating this afternoon. I'm sure this isn't the best time to talk. Maybe we could try this again later."

"Oh, sure," Tori said. "Later. Sure. How much later? Another thirteen years?"

Without waiting to hear her father's reply, Tori turned and ran back to the hotel.

The ladies' locker room was hushed, but there was an electric feeling in the air.

This is it, Tori thought grimly, the long program, my last chance to win a medal. She looked around the room and saw Jill looking at her. Both of them lowered their eyes. After everything that had happened last night and now this morning with her father, Tori didn't know what to say to her friend. She could tell Jill was at a loss too.

"I wish you two would make up," Danielle whispered to Tori. "Jill feels awful, I know she does."

"If she feels so awful, she can tell me herself," Tori whispered back. She hadn't meant to sound nasty—it was just so hard to say she was sorry. "Listen,

Danielle," she added in a softer tone. "I really don't want to talk about Jill now, okay?"

Danielle nodded and left Tori alone.

Tori stretched her legs and glanced around the room again. This time she saw Carla Benson watching her. Carla didn't lower her eyes, the way Jill had. Instead she strutted over to Tori and said, "So, Tori. When do you leave for Colorado?"

Tori hadn't told anyone yet that the so-called scout was actually her father. And she certainly wasn't about to mention it to Carla Benson, her arch-rival. "Who said I was going to Colorado?" she asked.

"You did," Carla said. "You've been bragging about it ever since we got here practically."

Tori tossed her head. "What's the matter, Carla? Are you jealous?"

"Ha!" Carla put her hands on her hips and leaned close to Tori. "You know what I think?" she said. "I think you made the whole thing up."

"Why would I do that?"

"To cover up for not being as good as you think you are," Carla said.

Tori laughed. "We'll see who's good, Carla," she said. "When you're watching me get a medal later, we'll see who's really good."

Tori thought that Carla was about to say more, but there wasn't time. Carla had to go warm up on the ice, and so did Jill. Tori watched them both leave, then started to get dressed herself.

As Tori sat on one of the benches to lace up her skates, her mother came in. Tori turned away from her, bracing herself for the usual flurry of orders to hurry and adjust her dress, and start warming up. Instead Mrs. Carsen sat on one of the benches and started reading a travel brochure she'd picked up at the hotel. She hadn't been happy about Tori's meeting her father, and Tori guessed she was still angry about it and about everything that had happened during the trip.

Tori went over to one of the full-length mirrors to check her appearance. In the glass she could see her mom, still sitting there quietly. Her mother hadn't asked about the meeting with her dad, but Tori knew she must be dying to know.

Her mother seemed sad—and even a bit lost. Suddenly Tori's anger melted. "I yelled at him," she said.

Mrs. Carsen looked up from the brochure. There was a surprised expression on her face. "At your father?"

Tori nodded. "I didn't mean to, but I was upset. I guess it wasn't such a good idea to meet him before I skated."

Her mother made a sound that resembled a snort. "I could have told you that," she said.

Tori sighed. "I know, Mom. You were probably right. About that. But not about everything."

Mrs. Carsen looked at the clock. "Tori, I hardly think this is the time to be having this conversation."

"There you go again," Tori said. "See? All I want is

for you to let me decide a few things by myself. And I think I can have this conversation and still skate well, so why don't you let me?"

It was her mother's turn to sigh. "All right. Go on."

"I'm just about finished anyway," Tori said. "What I've been trying to tell you is that I want you to leave me alone sometimes. I don't mean forever or all the time," she added quickly. "I just want some space, that's all. And I want your support too." Tori meant it. As angry as she'd been earlier, she'd actually missed not having her mother around at practice. If only her mother could be there and be quiet.

Mrs. Carsen stuffed the brochure in her pocketbook and stood up. "I don't think we should try to resolve all this now," she said, giving Tori a quick hug. "But one thing's for certain—you'll always have my support."

They left the locker room together, and Mrs. Carsen went to take her seat for the program. Tori felt a little better about things. She and her mother would probably argue about this a hundred more times, but at least they'd started talking about it.

Tori knew that this was what Jill had been trying to tell her all along. She hadn't been jealous about the scout or the newspaper article. She'd felt sorry for Tori.

After her warm-up on the ice, Tori sat in the hall outside the arena, stretching and shaking her arms and legs to keep them from tightening. Her mind was almost completely focused on her program, until Carla

Benson appeared in the hall. The photographer from the newspaper was on her heels, snapping a picture.

Carla must have just finished, Tori thought as the Blade Runners skater strode past her. Carla didn't even glance at Tori, but Tori could see she wasn't happy. There was always a lot of pressure on the skater who was in first place going into the long program. Had Carla skated a bad program and ruined her chances to bring home the gold?

A few minutes later Tori heard a burst of applause from inside the arena. Jill was after Carla—the crowd must be clapping for Jill.

But now it was Tori's turn, and she shoved everyone and everything out of her mind as she stepped onto the ice. She had to concentrate on herself. She had to skate her best.

Tori stood poised, waiting for the opening notes of the song "Somewhere" from the musical *West Side Story* to begin her program. The music started, and Tori lifted her right leg high into a spiral and glided the length of the ice. Suddenly she turned and circled the rink with powerful backward crossovers. She held her breath and prepared for her difficult jump combination—a double Lutz into a double loop. Tori knew she had to land these jumps if she wanted the rest of the program to go smoothly.

Just as she was ready to go into the combination, Tori saw a man sitting in the front row of the bleachers. Her father had come to watch her skate. Tori hesitated for a fraction of a second. Mr. Weiler was always lecturing her and the other members of Silver Blades about the importance of concentration. If she wanted to be a real skater and compete in the Olympics someday, she couldn't let her emotions get in her way.

Barely missing a beat, Tori reached back and planted her right toepick in the ice. She hoped the judges hadn't noticed her slight falter. She launched herself into the air and pulled her arms and legs in tight, rotating twice. She landed cleanly and with her right knee bent enough so that she immediately sprang off her right blade into a double loop jump. She landed the jump solidly. She'd done it!

But there was no time for self-congratulations. Tori completed a flying camel spin, in which she pulled her leg high above her head, and an axel–double toe loop combination, and then began her intricate footwork pattern in time to the music. Her footwork brought her down the side of the rink where the nine judges sat. Tori concentrated on keeping her head up and trying to make eye contact with the judges, as well as with the audience. Her heart was pounding.

Tori performed her double axel, flying sitspin, and double flip flawlessly. She connected each required move with beautiful choreography that highlighted the melody of the music. Tori felt herself becoming Maria, the star of *West Side Story,* and she skated as if the music were written just for her.

Three minutes and thirty seconds after she began, Tori breathlessly completed her final layback spin. When she heard the applause, she knew she'd come very close to skating her best.

"**Y**ou were great!" Kerry Morris cried to Tori in the locker room. "Third place! Congratulations!"

"Thanks," Tori said. She was disappointed, but she didn't show it. Her scores for the long program had been better than Carla's. Carla had missed two jumps and almost fallen on a third. But her scores from the short program were so good that she stayed ahead of Tori, in second place.

"Jill!" Tori heard Nikki cry. "Fantastic! First place, can you believe it! I'm so happy for you!"

"I really *can't* believe it yet," Jill said with a grin. "Maybe when the medal's around my neck."

Tori looked away. Jill had skated beautifully, with the best scores of the day. Combined with her scores from the short program, she'd moved ahead of Carla, and in a little while she'd be wearing the gold medal.

"Hey, Tori," Nikki said, giving her a hug. "How come you're looking so down? You won the bronze! You should be cheering!"

"We all should," said Danielle, who'd placed fifth. "Silver Blades took two out of the three medals in the junior ladies' singles. And Gary Hernandez took the bronze in men's, and wait until Nikki and Alex are ready for competition. We'll have even more medals!"

"So cheer up, Tori," Nikki said.

"I'm not unhappy, really," Tori said. "I'm just a little mad at myself. If I hadn't gotten so shook up during my short program, I could have done better." She nodded at Carla and lowered her voice. "I really wanted to beat her," she whispered.

"Next time," Danielle said with a grin as Carla left the locker room.

"Right," Tori agreed with determination. "Next time." Tori glanced at Jill. She wanted to congratulate her, but she still felt awkward.

Just then Mrs. Carsen swept into the locker room. "Tori, you were marvelous!" she cried. "You see what concentration can do for you? If only your short—"

"I know, Mom," Tori interrupted.

Mrs. Carsen stopped talking for a moment. "You're right," she finally said. "I'm sure you do know." She gave Tori a hug, then headed toward the door. "I'm going to get back to my seat," she said. "I've got my camera, so be sure to smile and stand up straight at the medal ceremony, Tori."

Tori shook her head as Mrs. Carsen went out the door. It would be a long time before her mother gave up telling her what to do.

"Hey, look at this," Nikki said. She'd found a newspaper on one of the benches and was holding it up. "It's the article that reporter was doing."

Jill, Danielle, and Tori gathered around. Tori gasped when she saw the headline. BLADE RUNNERS' CARLA BENSON—A YOUNG SKATER'S STORY.

"Carla Benson!" Jill cried. "That reporter interviewed me for an hour! What happened?"

"You're in here, Jill," Nikki said, scanning the article. "It says 'Jill Wong of Silver Blades agrees with Carla that the triple toe loop is one of the hardest jumps.'"

"And?" Jill said.

"And nothing," Nikki said. "That's all. It's all about Carla."

"I can't believe it!" Jill looked disgusted.

Tori laughed. Jill whirled toward her, but Tori shook her head. "I'm sorry, I'm not laughing at you," Tori said. "It's just kind of funny, that's all. I mean, I bet that reporter is furious with herself."

"Right," Danielle agreed. "She obviously doesn't know how to pick a winner."

Jill started laughing too. "Yeah. Who cares about a

newspaper story when you've got a medal around your neck?" She smiled at Tori. "Right?"

"Right," Tori said.

"And a scout from Colorado interested in you," Jill said.

Tori blushed. "Well. That would be great, but it's not happening."

"Don't tell me your mother said no," Jill said.

Tori shook her head. "My mother didn't know anything about a scout, because there isn't a scout."

"Then who was that guy?" Nikki asked.

Just then Mrs. Carsen stuck her head in the door. "Tori," she said, "your father wants to talk to you. I told him it was up to you." She smiled and disappeared.

"Your father?" Danielle said. "What is she talking about? You don't even know him."

"That's right," Tori said. "I just met him. He's the scout."

"Huh?" Jill said.

"He's the guy who kept watching me," Tori explained sheepishly. "He's not a scout; he's my father. He lives here, and he saw my picture and he wanted to meet me. We talked this morning, but . . . " Her voice trailed off. "I guess I wasn't ready."

"This is amazing!" Nikki cried.

"Tell me about it," Tori agreed.

"So, are you going to talk to him again?" Jill asked eagerly.

"Well, you heard my mother. She left it up to me." Tori grinned at Jill.

"It's about time," Jill said, putting her arm around her friend.

"Thanks," Tori said softly. "I know that's what you were trying to tell me." She gave her three friends a warm smile. "See you guys later. I need to talk to my father before the medal ceremony begins."

Tori found her father waiting in the hall outside the locker room. Her mother was nowhere in sight. "Hi," she said.

Mr. Carsen turned around, smiling nervously. "Hi, Tori," he said. "I'm glad you decided to see me."

Tori was still in her skating dress, but she'd put on sneakers and her warm-up jacket. "You want to walk again?" she asked.

"It's up to you," her father said.

Tori smiled to herself. In the last few hours she'd had the chance to make a few of her own decisions and it felt great. "I'm famished," she said. "There's a snack bar in the arena. Why don't we go eat something?"

"Fine."

The two of them walked silently through the halls until they found the snack bar. Tori ordered a cheese-burger. Her father had coffee.

"Congratulations, by the way," Mr. Carsen said, sitting at a table. "You must be proud of yourself, winning a medal."

"I am," Tori said. "I could have done better, though."

"I don't see how. I thought you looked perfect. I watched you skate, you know."

Tori nodded. "I saw you. I saw you the first time, too, in my short program. That's when I thought you were scouting me."

"Doing what?" he asked.

Tori's cheeseburger came, and as she put ketchup on it, she explained how she'd thought he was a scout from the famous training school in Colorado.

Mr. Carsen laughed. "Sorry to disappoint you. I just came because I wanted to see you."

Tori didn't know what to say. She couldn't deny she'd been disappointed that there hadn't been a scout, but now it didn't matter quite as much. After years of imagining who her father was, what he looked like, the type of job he did, here he was across the table from her And he had sought her out and tried to make contact with her. She ate some of her cheeseburger, then said, "I'm sorry I was kind of nasty before."

"Well, you had a right to be," her father said. "I'm sure it's upsetting to have somebody suddenly appear in your life after all this time."

Tori nodded. "It is," she agreed. "Why did you leave? Was it me? Was it having a baby? I mean, how awful was I?"

"Is that what you think, Tori?" Mr. Carsen looked upset. "Is that what your mother told you?"

Tori shook her head. She felt like crying again. "Mom never told me anything really, except that you had left. I always thought it was because of me, though."

Now her father looked sad. "It didn't have anything to do with you," he said. "I hope you'll believe me, because it's true. Your mother and I . . . well, I met her when she was trying to find something to do with her life besides skating. Skating didn't work out for her."

"I know," Tori said. She thought back to the conversation with her mother during the car ride up to Lake Placid—that was the first time she really understood why her mother pushed her so hard to succeed.

"Anyway," Mr. Carsen went on, "she was determined to be a success at something. And she was, at the design business. I was glad for her, but after you were born, I hardly ever saw her. She was either working or busy with you. I just wanted . . . I don't know. Something different, I guess. So I left, without even telling her why or staying in touch with you." He shook his head ruefully. "That was wrong. But as I said this morning, I was young. And it's best that your mother and I didn't stay together, because when we did talk, we mostly argued. I think we're both happier now. But I shouldn't have left the two of you that way. And my leaving had absolutely nothing to do with you."

This time tears of relief welled up in Tori's eyes. She brushed them away, grateful that her father didn't make any remarks about them. Everything seemed to be changing so fast. She still didn't fully understand why he'd left, but at least now maybe she wouldn't wonder all the time if it had been because of her.

"When I saw your picture in the paper," her father went on, "I just had to see you. And when I watched you skate, I was so proud. I wanted to tell everybody you were my daughter, but I realized I didn't have any bragging rights. I knew I couldn't miss this chance to meet you."

Tori finished her cheeseburger, and they talked awhile longer. He told her about his work as an architect, and about his wife—he'd remarried eight years earlier. She told him a little about school and her skating.

"Listen, Tori," Mr. Carsen said fifteen minutes later. "I know you don't want to stay here long. It must be almost time for the medal ceremony."

Tori looked at the clock. "I've got about half an hour," she said.

This is pretty awkward, so maybe we shouldn't try to say too much at once," he went on. "I just want to tell you that I think your mother's done a fine job of bringing you up. You're bright, you're talented, and you seem like a great girl." He laughed. "You get part of the credit, too, of course."

"Thanks," Tori said quietly.

He looked at her with a serious expression.

"We don't know each other at all," he said, "so I don't expect you to start suddenly thinking of me as your father."

That was good, Tori thought, because she couldn't. In her eyes he was still a stranger.

"I'd like to get to know you, but only if you want to," Mr. Carsen said. "Maybe we could write to each other once in a while. And then maybe we could telephone or visit each other. But all you have to do is say the word and I'll stay out of your life."

He was leaving it up to her. This was another decision for her to make on her own.

Tori sat in silence for a moment. This was one choice she couldn't make right away, she realized. It was way too soon for her to think about visiting her father, but writing letters might be a good start. Finally she told her father that she wanted to think about it, and she carefully watched his face.

"That's fine, Tori," he said gently. "I understand. In the meantime, here's my address and phone number."

She took the piece of paper he'd scribbled on, and stared at his name: James Carsen. She still couldn't believe she'd come all this way to skate in a Regional competition and wound up meeting her father. She shook her head. It was like a dream.

Then, tucking the paper into the pocket of her jacket, she stood up. "I'd better go get ready for the ceremony," she said with a smile. "Maybe you'd like to come watch it."

"Yes, I would," her father said, smiling back at her. "Thank you, Tori."

15

Ten minutes later Tori stood in the waiting area with Jill and Carla. Carla didn't say anything to either of them, and Tori was just as glad.

"How's my hair?" Jill asked.

"It's fine," Tori said. "You look great."

"Thanks," Jill said. "I guess I'm afraid I'll fall on my way out there."

"So what?" Tori said. "It's too late. They can't take the medal away from you."

There was an awkward pause. Jill probably thinks I'm angry at her for beating me, Tori thought. The truth was, she was jealous; she couldn't help it. But she wasn't angry, and she wanted her friend to know it. "Listen, Jill," she said. "This may not be the best time to say this, but I want to apologize to you."

"For what?" Jill said.

Tori smiled. "You know perfectly well what for. For the way I've acted through this whole competition. I— I guess the tension just got to me. But I hated fighting with you. I really care about you."

Jill smiled back. "I know you do," she said. "I think I owe you an apology too. I wasn't exactly sweetness and light, you know."

The two girls hugged. Suddenly a voice boomed over the loudspeakers, "Winner of the bronze medal! Miss Tori Carsen!"

"Go get it, Tori!" Jill said, punching Tori lightly on the shoulder.

Head high, a smile on her face, Tori stepped onto the ice and skated toward the center of the rink. She heard the applause and saw Nikki and Danielle, and Alex and Melinda and a bunch of other kids from Silver Blades. She saw her mother clapping like crazy. She saw her father, too, not far from her mother, grinning and giving her a thumbs-up sign.

In the center of the rink were three round podiums. The one in the middle was higher than the other two. That was where Jill would stand. Tori skated to a stop at the left podium and stepped onto it. An official from the skating association walked up to her, and Tori bent her head slightly as he slipped the medal over her neck. She shook his hand, and the crowd clapped loudly. Tori could see flashbulbs going off, and she smiled and waved.

Carla Benson's name was called next, and Carla skated to the podium on the right and got her silver medal. To be polite, Tori clapped along with the crowd.

"Miss Jill Wong!" the loudspeaker boomed. Jill skated out and got onto the higher middle podium. The official put the gold medal around her neck, and this time Tori didn't have to pretend to be happy. She was glad for Jill, and she was really glad they'd made up. Jill was too good a friend to lose.

The crowd applauded loudly, and the girls waved and smiled. Tori and Jill hugged each other. Carla kept waving to the crowd.

"It's over," Jill said. "I can't believe it. It felt so good getting that medal, I wish the feeling could last forever."

"There'll be other times," Tori said. Of course, next time she planned to be the one winning the gold.

"Come on," Jill said, "let's go change and do something fun."

"Like meeting a bunch of high school guys at Mirror Lake, maybe?" Tori asked with a giggle.

Laughing, the two friends started to step down when somebody shouted, "Hey, nice going, you two!" It was Barbara Nolan, the reporter. She was leaning over the barrier. Next to her was the photographer. "Listen," she called, "I'd like Max to get a shot of you for the paper, okay?"

"Sure!" Tori said immediately.

"All three of you," Ms. Nolan called. "Lean close together and look thrilled."

As Tori and Jill climbed back onto the podiums, Jill whispered, "Can you manage to look thrilled when Carla's so close?"

"I'm not sure," Tori whispered back. "Maybe you could hold up two fingers, like a pitchfork, behind her head right before Max takes the picture."

"Cool," Jill agreed.

"Okay, girls!" the reporter interrupted. "Smile!"

As Tori stood there on the lowest podium, she realized to her surprise that she didn't mind not being the center of attention. Actually it felt great to be wearing a medal and sharing the spotlight with Jill—and even with Carla Benson. Tori didn't like the other skater very much, but she had to admit that Carla was talented.

After the photographer snapped the photo, Tori looked into the crowd. Among the sea of people she saw Nikki and Danielle in their light blue jackets. They were jumping up and down and waving like mad.

"Yay, way to go, Silver Blades," yelled Nikki.

"Two medals for Silver Blades!" shouted Danielle.

Tori grinned and waved back to her two friends.

Meet the Silver Blades Skaters . . .

Nikki, Danielle, Tori, and Jill are four talented skaters who share one special dream—competing in the Olympics someday. And they're going to try to make it all happen in Silver Blades, the best skating club around!

Don't miss any of the other books in
the Silver Blades series:

#1: Breaking the Ice

Nikki Simon is thrilled when she makes the Silver Blades skating club. But Nikki quickly realizes that being a member of Silver Blades is going to be tougher than she thought. Both Nikki and another skater, Tori Carsen, have to land the double flip jump. But how far will Tori go to make sure that she lands it first?

#2: In the Spotlight

Danielle Panati has always worked hard at her skating, and it's definitely starting to pay off. Danielle's just won the lead role in the Silver Blades Fall Ice Spectacular. Rehearsals go well at first, then the other members of Silver Blades start noticing that Danielle is acting strange. Is it the pressure of being in the spotlight— or does Danielle have a secret that she doesn't want to share?

and coming soon . . .

#4: Going for the Gold

The coaches from a famous figure-skating center in Colorado want Jill Wong to move there to train to be a national champion. Jill's always dreamed about this kind of opportunity, but now that it's here, she can't imagine moving thousands of miles away from her family and best friends. Is her skating worth such a big sacrifice?